Duncan's sea... takes him to the West Indies.

Tropical Cocktales with a Twist

Tales of Old Barbados

KAY GILLESPIE

LMH
LMH Publishing Limited

All LMH titles, imprints and distributed lines are available at special quantity discounts for bulk purchases for sales promotion, premiums, fund-raising, educational or institutional use.

Consultant Executive Editor: Julia Tan

Copy Editor: Julia Tan (Singapore)

Cover Design; Susan Lee-Quee

Book Design, Layout & Typesetting: Michelle M. Mitchell

Published by: LMH Publishing Limited
7 Norman Road,
LOJ Industrial Complex
Building 10
Kingston C.S.O., Jamaica
Tel: 876-938-0005; 938-0712
Fax: 876-759-8752
Email: lmhbookpublishing@cwjamaica.com
Website: www.lmhpublishingjamaica.com

Printed in the U.S.A.   ISBN 976-8184-42-6

AUTHOR'S NOTE

If you think you can tell the difference between truth and reality, the supernatural and dreams; want to find out who you really are, where you come from? Why not visit the beautiful island of Barbados but don't just lie on the beach, take Duncan's map with you and see if you can discover the truth. Perhaps nothing is real but maybe, just maybe you will discover what is. If you bump into Duncan, give him a hug for me.

Kay Gillespie

DUNCAN'S SKETCH MAP

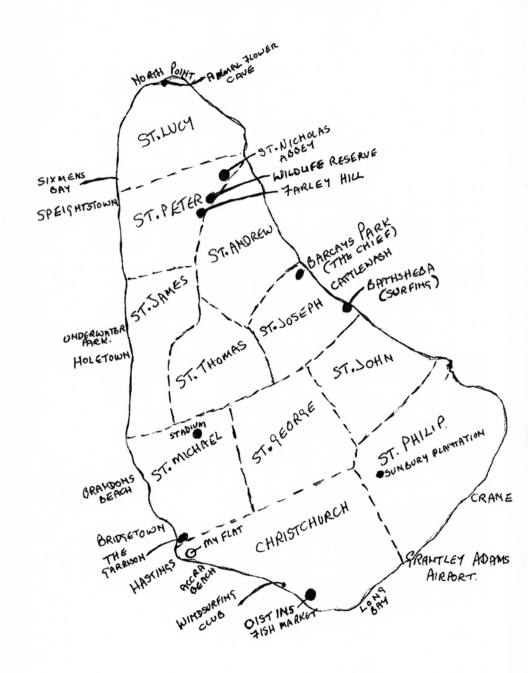

CONTENTS

BURIED TREASURE

Would you like to know where treasure is found?
Where the sky meets the sea, where magic abounds?
Take flight to the island called Petit Angleterre,
Answer the riddles when you arrive there.

Where the tallest mahogany bow to the sea,
Where the heavens rain pods making intruders flee.
Pearly white gates open wide for just you,
No parrots live here, but one will call through.

The house in the trees and the trees in the house,
It's here where the treasure lies, quiet as a mouse.
Where schools of fish swim yet never move fin,
Fruit that looks sweet, but know you can't eat.

Exotic Birds of Paradise dwell nearby,
But their stares are wooden and they can't fly.
The treasure is yours, you have it already,
So come, stake a claim, it's held for you steady.

No diamonds, no gold, yet its worth is untold,
The essence of life is yours to unfold.
Look deep in your loved one's eyes and see
The answer lies there, for eternity.

DUNCAN STUART

"Ooh I'm going to Barbados,
Gem of the Caribbean Sea.
Ooh I'm going to Barbados,
da de da de da de..."

It's no good, I can't stop that old song going round and round inside my head. Just wish I knew the rest of the words. It's driving me crazy! Oh, by the way my name is Duncan Stuart. I am sitting at Gatwick Airport with my third cup of coffee enjoying the hustle and bustle around me, marvelling at the sights and agitated sounds of distraught people wanting to get away from it all and relax. Most of them look tired and grumpy due to several delays. In fact, my own flight has been put back two hours but nothing could dampen my sense of excitement. No, it's more than that, more a sense of something incredible about to happen. I am off on an adventure, a quest even. I don't care if I have to wait twenty four hours for it to begin, after all I've already waited twenty six years, what's a few more hours. Oh, oh, now the guilt is with me again, it always hits in those rare moments when forgetfulness comes and I'm happiest. Then it creeps round the corner and knocks me over the head with a sledgehammer. Does the pain ever stop being so sharp? But let me begin from the significant part of my youth.

Since leaving school I have worked in a bank; lucky to get the job really but then my father had worked there loyally all his life, so when he put his only son's name forward for a position, they readily accepted me. I had always wanted and assumed that I would go to art college or take a course in journalism, as painting and writing were the only subjects that ever held my interest. Oh the take for granted idealism of youth, I can hear you say. But you see, I had this romantic notion of becoming a top investigative reporter or an artist, who would spend long hot summers in Tuscany painting luscious nude females who would all fall madly in love with me. Never in my wildest nightmares did I think I would end up wearing a grey suit, and working in a dull office with the faceless ones but then I hadn't reckoned on Dad getting ill and another wage becoming essential. To say that I hated every single day of my working life would be an understatement; the tedious monotony, the pettiness of impotent rank-pulling by clerks only slightly older and less spotty than me. My only escape was to dream and my dreams were magnificent. On my way to work every morning, as I passed a travel shop, I would pick up a brochure of far-away places. I would place this in my top drawer, which I left half open, so that it seemed I was poring over my work-laden desk. In reality, I was inside my drawer flying off to every exotic location in the magazine. Inside my mind I had the most thrilling adventures and life was made more bearable living vicariously through the photographer's lens.

I was promoted slowly but surely and when my father died, it was expected that I would be given his position. I fully intended telling them what they could do with their jobs but things didn't quite turn out that way and it would be a few more years before I got to utter those words. I'd helped my mother look after Dad for several years. He had been a huge man and even though the weight had fallen off him he was too much for my mother alone to manage. Consequently, while my juvenile counterparts at the bank were exploring pubs, clubs and any nubile young girl they could get their hands on, I was turning Dad over, cleaning him up and generally taking over from Mum who was exhausted by the end of every day. He'd been a strong, proud man, and the fact that his only son had to perform these tasks I think got to him more than the cancer. Then, a little more than a year after his death, Mum was stricken with the same thing. When towards the end of her illness, things got rough, I was given sick leave to look after her. In those final months together, I honestly believe we became closer than we'd ever been before. I think maybe it was because we were free of having to think of Dad's needs all the time and could concentrate on each other. It was a caring, loving time. We both loved books; thrillers were our favourites and I enjoyed reading the latest one aloud to her. We had long conversations as I sat by the bed holding her hand and I got to know and admire the woman who was my mother. I had always loved her but now we became friends.

She told me about the Scottish grand-parents and great grand-parents who my own father had never mentioned, and at last I knew where I got my wandering spirit, my zest for a life that seemed unattainable. My great great grandfather had apparently travelled the world and lived for many years in the Caribbean, eventually overseeing a large sugar plantation in Barbados. I asked Mum how she had gleaned this information and she sent me up to the loft to fetch an old chest. It held letters and photographs, a record of my Scottish ancestry, which we spent hours poring over. I was amazed. Here was a family that I'd known nothing about. Having always imagined that I came from a long line of boring pen pushers, it sparked my interest to find out more; now I knew that my genes were made for adventure. I asked why my father had never spoken of his family but Mum said all Dad knew was that there had been a big falling out in his great great grandfather's time after which his great grandfather had left Scotland and his family for good, refusing to make contact or respond to their overtures ever again. Sporadic correspondence arrived over the generations, all of which were committed to the chest in the loft. Eventually a solicitor's letter arrived informing my grandfather that the last of the family had died leaving a small inheritance, and a few heirlooms which were also consigned to the loft. My tight-lipped father had never, as far as Mum knew, even looked inside the chest and when she confronted him about it, he said, "If my father and grandfather wanted nothing to do with them, then that's good enough for me!" All I can say is, it must have been one hell of a row!

Short dark days and interminable nights hung over me like storm clouds until I wished it all over, for both our sakes. Yet finally, when the end came I was devastated. After a solitary vigil at my Mother's funeral I came back to an empty quiet house and sat in silence, feeling such incredible loneliness. I was lost without her. She was at last out of her misery but mine continued. She smiled her small smile from familiar places where she lingered persistently until I could sense her pulling me with her. For the past year, my every thought had been of her. What special something could I prepare to tempt her palate? What flowers to put beside her bed? What story to read? When I went shopping I looked for little surprises to bring her. Always when I returned there had been her sweet smile to greet me, and it was that smile I saw now, in her bedroom, on the stairs, from the settee in the lounge. It was several weeks before the leaden ache inside began to ease and I finally pulled myself together, mainly because I remembered our chats. The way she had urged me to follow my dreams and travel to some of those exotic places in the brochures. It was time I made my move. I began by gathering all my parents' clothes for the old folks home.

Having stored the personal family belongings and arranged for the house to be rented, I walked on to the bank, stopping to pick up every brochure I could lay my hands on about the West Indies, especially Barbados. When I knocked on the manager's door and handed in my notice, he was understandably annoyed but I figured Dad and I had given enough of our lives to the bank. I packed a hold-all containing a few essentials, bought a ticket for Barbados and here I am at Gatwick. The adventure has begun.

"Lord, you smilin' like de cat that got de cream. You goin' to Barbados I see young man." A very large lady had sat down opposite me with a plate of chicken and chips and while reading my bag labels she proceeded to dig in. I closed my journal and put the pen down.

"Yes I am. It's my first time abroad. My name's Duncan Stuart by the way." I offered my hand.

She wiped her fingers on the napkin and took it. Her hand felt soft and delicate in mine.

"I'm Cecily Ward, nice to meet you. Well, Duncan you have picked the most beautiful spot in the world for your first trip. I should know, I live there. I'm a Barbadian." She opened two more sachets of tomato sauce and emptied them over her remaining chips. 'I've spent six weeks with my sister in England and I feel that my bones are never goin' to be warm again. But I had a good time you know; good to see the nieces and nephews and do some shopping at Marks and Spencer. Still an' all I'm longing for some chicken wings that taste like chicken; those British birds, they got no flavour, must a been made in a fact'ry!"

Her smile was infectious and between mouthfuls we continued our conversation until she cleared her plate. Incredibly I found myself telling her my life story, such as it was.

"Lord boy, you've had a bad time but never you mind; Bajan people gonna take you into their open arms and make you feel right at home. Now you give me your address where you're staying and once I'm seckled you can come over for some good Bajan cooking." She looked me over. "You could do with some meat on you!"

She smiled the warmest smile I had ever seen. At last our flight was called but I was disappointed to find that I wasn't sitting nearer Cecily; I didn't suppose I would ever see her again.

I had booked a window seat specially, so that I wouldn't miss a thing; I couldn't wait for the take off. A young woman placed a large bag on the seat beside me and was struggling with other assorted packages. I jumped up to help her put them in the overhead locker. They were extremely heavy and she saw my grimace.

"I know, they weigh a ton don't they? It's the booze and the funny part is, I hardly ever drink!"

Between us, we managed to fit them all in and sat down. "You're very kind, thank you..."
She waited for my name, then introduced herself. Her name was Sarah Patten. At that moment a very florid fat man arrived next to Sarah's aisle seat.

"Haven't you got settled yet Sarah? I honestly don't know what you do with yourself!" He looked at me and raised his eyes heaven wards. "Women! Can't do a thing without us can they?"
I was about to say that I didn't know how one person could carry so much when he turned again to Sarah.

"Have a good flight old girl. As I'm in first class I shall be out before you so I'll meet you in the car park." He turned immediately and made his way forward. Squeezing past a stewardess, he let his arm linger around her waist as he said in a loud voice, "Hope you've got your best champagne on ice for me in first class m'dear!"
We settled into our seats and I asked, "Is that your boss Sarah?"
"You could say that Duncan." She smiled, "Actually, Roger's my husband."
"But why is he..? Oh never mind, it's none of my business."
"Why is he in first class and I'm back here with the poor people?" She was smiling again. "The only reason I came on this trip with him was because my mother died suddenly in England. My heart lurched as she continued, "and I had to fly back to arrange the funeral, the house sale, oh and a million and one other things. Roger travels a lot for his off-shore company and they pick up all the bills; flights, fancy hotels, expensive dinners with clients, everything. Unfortunately, expenses never seem to stretch to his

wife, so he has to pay my fare out of his own pocket...well you know." She looked at me and there was that glint in her eyes again. "I swear if he could have found a large enough sea gull to carry this tonnage," she patted her tummy, "he'd have saddled it and put me on that!"

I didn't think she was large at all; curvy was the word I would use, an hour-glass figure they used to call it. Sarah looked about ten years older than me, mid-thirties I guessed, with brown eyes and blonde curly hair pinned on top of her head. She was very pretty. Were all the good women married I wondered? I'd spent so many years looking after my parents that there didn't seem any time for romance and now all the nice ones would probably be attached. Ah well, maybe on this trip I will be destined to meet the love of my life. No doubt about it, I am a true romantic.

Sarah was obviously amused when I paid rapt attention to the safety instructions and when the plane started moving, I thought I would explode with excitement. She had helped me fasten my seat belt and now we were speeding down the runway with everything flashing past. What a sensation! When we lifted off, we rose so unexpectedly and fast that instantly below us was a toy land of minute houses and cars. Sarah clasped my hand and only then did I realise how rigidly I'd been holding it.

"You don't mind do you, only I get a bit scared at take off and landings?" she said. I squeezed her hand but was sure she was just trying to be nice. How could this massive piece of metal lift itself off the ground and then stay airborne? How could it rise into the air so fast, so steeply? My heart had literally seemed to fly into my mouth. This was living! I felt exhilarated.

I took all the drinks and snacks that were offered and commiserated with Sarah about our mothers' deaths. I thought the meals the airline provided were delicious and ate everything, while Sarah made a face and said that she thought I must have lived a very sheltered life. I didn't argue with that. During the flight she told me all about Barbados and wrote down a list of places to go. She also gave me her telephone number. Soon after we finished watching the film, Sarah started dozing but my adrenalin kept me as fresh as a daisy for the whole trip.

At last the pilot's voice told us that he was beginning his descent into Barbados and said that the people on the port side of the plane would soon see land. As we flew over the island, Sarah explained the layout of the parishes. Then we were travelling parallel to the west coast and I was amazed at the beauty of the beaches and the colours of the sea. When we landed Sarah and I said our farewells in case we lost each other in the airport crowds. I felt I was saying goodbye to a real friend but we both promised to stay in touch. Unbelievably I'd made two friends already and I hadn't got off the plane yet! I stood for a moment at the top of the steps and felt as though someone had slapped me in the face with a hot wet flannel.

Then as we filed down I looked up at the impossibly blue sky with the scudding white clouds. 'Yes!' I thought, 'This is it! Hot, humid, exotic, beautiful Barbados!' Just in front of the customs hall a steel band was playing and guess what? They were playing 'Beautiful, Beautiful Barbados'. How about that for coincidence? And I had only just managed to get the song out of my mind.

As I waited in the mini bus for the other people bound for the same south coast hotel, I looked out of the window to the car park. Sarah was there, struggling towards a car with her bags and packages; inside the car sat her husband Roger waiting impatiently.

We left the airport and immediately local sights and sounds assailed my senses. We passed large expensive looking houses where Dennis, our driver, said, "The big ups live." Then it was down onto the coast road and a ride through the parish of Christchurch. Here we drove past little wooden chattel houses huddled at the roadside, some pretty, some run down and there were open bars where men sat drinking beer to the loud slapping of dominoes. Everywhere it seemed people were milling about laughing, shouting to each other, especially when we passed through Oistins fish market. Everything was so colourful, the blue sky, the intense sunlight bouncing off the multi-coloured dresses and shirts and I thought, why do we have dark rain coats in the U.K.? All right, it rains a lot but why not bright red, blue, orange or yellow ones, perhaps with brollys to match; it just might lighten peoples' moods back home. Dennis said Oistins was the very best place to get a fish meal.

As we neared the hotel, a beautiful expanse of sand opened up on the left, and the white tipped blue of the Caribbean Sea beyond, took my breath away. I was shown to my room overlooking Accra Beach, the one we had just passed but before I had time to unpack, there was a knock at the door. A waiter made a nice welcoming speech and presented me with a rum punch, the best drink I had ever tasted. I would become very fond of these. I sipped my drink, enjoying the view until I heard a scuttling sound in the room behind me. I twisted round at once, but couldn't see a thing. My imagination, however, gave what ever it was boots!

THE MAHOGANY BIRD

There is a jewel set in the Caribbean Sea,
Where golden sands stretch to blue infinity.
Come, take a look, don't take my word,
But please don't mention the Mahogany Bird.

Myriad blooms shouting colours to the sun,
Gentle humming birds fan and kiss each one.
Palm trees that dot this sugared land
Carry water gourds made by nature's hand.

From another era haughty lizards freeze, stretch high,
Pose, turn proud head and cast disdainful eye
As a hundred feet tap a wild tattoo,
The millipede is passing through.

Bruggadung! The sun sinks all too soon,
Derisive cockerels defy the moon.
Stars vie with fireflies for the night
While startled dark winged bats take flight.

As tree frogs whistle in Morse code
Crickets, cats and dogs explode
Joining the dark cacophony,
Do you hear the Mahogany?

Oh secret elusive Mahogany Bird,
Is your song too sweet to ever be heard?
Your gossamer flight too swift each mile?
And why do they speak your name and smile?

Some of the people from my flight were already in the bar when I arrived; showered, shaved and ready for fun. We were all in very high spirits and several rounds of rum punches later, were feeling no pain. Somebody noticed the silver metal sleeves around the palm trees and were horrified when Mark, the bar man, told us it was to stop the rats climbing into our bedrooms. He said we had to realise we were in the tropics now, that there were many creepy crawlies about. Then we noticed that the trees were full of fireflies, it was magical. I couldn't be sure but Monica from Newcastle seemed to be hitting on me, or was it just wishful thinking?

"Luckily for us in Barbados; unlike for instance, Trinidad, nothing is poisonous here." Mark paused. "Nothing that is except old forty leg; that's a centipede to you folks; he could give you a nasty bite. But you know, the worst of them all is the Mahogany Bird. You really have to be careful of that!" We all spoke at once. "What did it look like? What would it do to you? Can it kill you? Is there a cure?"

Mark hushed us all and said it was time for dinner. He would give us the information we wanted after the meal.

Everyone asked their waiters about the Mahogany Birds but they just smiled and said we would soon find out. The meal was simple but so tasty that we all cleared our plates. The fish was fresh and spicy, the chicken tasted divine and there was sweet potato pie, macaroni cheese and christophene, all generously covered with a thick dark gravy. Coconut pie and ice cream followed.

Back at the bar, we were just getting stuck into our third round of rum punch when one of the women let out a terrible shriek. A massive cockroach had landed in her hair. She was nearly hysterical before we managed at last to dislodge it. Behind the bar, Mark was in fits of laughter. When he could draw breath he told us all that we had met our first Mahogany Bird! Boy you should have seen that big old roach, I swear you could have put a saddle on him. It was the early hours before we called it a night but sleep evaded me as I found it necessary to get up and investigate every sound. Eventually I closed my eyes, without envisaging yet another giant gruesome creature filling my dark world and slept.

The next morning I was up and on the beach before the rest of my new friends were awake. I ran into the blue sea and swam out before diving beneath the waves, going deep, holding my breath for as long as I could, then heading for the surface, through sunlit water sparkling like diamonds, lungs bursting. I rode on the waves and swam out again. At last I was exhausted and lay on the sand feeling the warm sun on my back. This was heaven; I didn't want to move; I felt like a king living on his own wonderful island and those sorry souls in their grey suits seemed a lifetime away. I lay there feeling incredibly relaxed, almost a sensation of floating.

After a while I made myself get up, simply because I was ravenous and breakfast would soon be served. Wrapping a towel around my middle, I stood at the side of the road waiting to cross. There was very little traffic but I watched as a rickety old push bike came towards me. It was ridden by an old man in a rather stained pink suit. He wore white gloves, a bow tie, hat and lace up shoes. He was the thinnest man I had ever seen. As he passed I noticed a pipe sticking out of his top pocket and the old fellow put his fingers up to his hat in a gentlemanly greeting. I said 'Good morning' and he rode slowly onwards. I knew I was just going to love it here; everybody was so friendly.

Over breakfast a couple of the guys said they were going to hire a moke and drive out to Banks Brewery. Mark had told them that a special masters tournament cricket match was being held in the grounds and he asked if I would like to make up a foursome. I needed little urging when he told us some of the old West Indies greats would be putting in an appearance; Sir Garfield Sobers, Wes Hall, Charlie Grifiths and Joel Garner; Mark said Courtney Walsh and Curtley Ambrose were rumoured to be attending too but then added, "Bajans love to spread a lickle gossip so that may not be true!" On our way to the match, Mark handed round some pieces of freshly cut sugar cane for us to chew, which was so sweet my mouth's juicing up, just remembering it. Now I realised why the milk on our cereal had tasted so good.

When we arrived at the tiny sports ground right next to the brewery, we all sat down at the edge of the boundary, as close as possible to the wicket. Mark had warned that we would be frazzled by the ten o'clock sun but with a case of cold beers and the Banks Eleven already facing a few overs against a local team to warm the audience up, we were heeding no warnings. One of the bowlers was outstanding and making mincemeat of the opposition. He was a chubby man, middle aged with a bald pate which shone in the sun and was covered by a huge plaster. We started batting ideas to and fro as to how the bowler had received his injury when a local man sitting nearby on the grass, overheard the conversation.

"That would be Dennis' missus, Cheryl! Lord, with a missus like that one, we'd all be singing soprano!" He broke off, laughing with his friends and nudging each other.

One and then another of them would remember some incident concerning the couple and more guffaws of laughter would break out. "Mind you," the man became serious and his friends were still, "she hot though nah?"

They nodded, ooh-ed in agreement and went back to watching the game but every so often one of the men would slap his thigh recalling another story about Dennis and Cheryl. Their voices became fainter as the heat and beer brought a lethargy that pulled my eye lids closed, much as I fought against it.

HEAVEN CAN WAIT

Cheryl woke to the sound of bird song and a wonderful feeling of well-being. The aroma of freshly ground coffee filled her nostrils as she stretched and ran her hands over her well-toned body, feeling pleasure in the hardening muscles. There was a faint sound of digging coming from the garden and she smiled as she realised Dennis was hard at work there as ordered. In Cheryl's opinion gardening and cricket were the only two things her husband was any good at. His grateful cricket team had given him complimentary tickets, for the test match, at Kensington Oval today but she told him last night that he had work to do, so his friends would have to go without him. The women's club meeting was being held in Cheryl's home in five days' time and the garden had to be as spick and span as the house for her ladies. Cheryl told Dennis that Kensington could wait until his jobs were done. He had stared at her for a minute, then turned resignedly to open the garden door, head bowed muttering something under his breath.

"What did you say?"

"Nothing, nothing. It doesn't matter."

The familiar red started somewhere in the top of her head and seeped down over her eyes. "Don't you dare lie to me! Nothing is it?" She moved in on him fast, picking up her discarded shoe from a chair. "You useless heap of nothing!"

Dennis tried to close the door between them but Cheryl was strong and pulled it open with her right hand. The left hand, brought the shoe with its five inch steel tipped heel, crashing down on his head. He staggered back into the garden, dizzy and spurting blood.

Lying in bed now and remembering, Cheryl had to laugh. He'd looked so ridiculous. Twenty years she had been married to Dennis and it had been like a prison sentence, what an almighty bore he was. The only time he went out was to church or to a game of cricket. They rarely went out together; she thought it reflected badly on her to be seen with such a wimp and most certainly never to church; far too many people. Anyway, as she was so fond of telling him, "Heaven can wait, there's too much living to do!" There was no sex any more, not with him anyway. She smiled remembering "Abs", the trainer at the gym and her lover for the past two years. She touched herself remembering the feel of him, ooh man was he hot. When their sweat covered bodies were straining together and she was pulling his thighs onto hers, she always yelled, "Do it Abs! Do it to me!" Tyrone liked to be called by his nickname. Not only did he think it was macho but if the women didn't know his real name, there was less chance of his wife finding out. But, as Cheryl told her friends, when she was grasping her hands round his hard round little botsie, all she could think of was 'those tight buns and the hugeness of him thrusting inside her!' She made the girls laugh and sigh with envy. He was always asking what they were giggling about when they watched him working out. Oh boy, heaven sure could wait until she got tired of her "Abs" man.

When they first married, the pair of them were at it like rabbits; any time, any where, any place. Then she got pregnant. Cheryl was horrified and decided to have an abortion. There was no way she was giving up her future career as an accountant to look after some little brat. Dennis had begged and pleaded pathetically for the life of their child, promising to put his law career on hold while he stayed home and cared for the baby, stupid man. He had been a top student too, yet he was prepared to give up all his ambitions for an unborn child. What an idiot! So they had a baby girl and he was as good as his promise, doing everything for the child while Cheryl resumed her career. He never did get a chance to go back

to law and instead got a job as a store manager which is where he still was. Sooo boring! She stretched again. Their daughter Maria had married a wealthy Englishman a year ago and they were now living in Kent. She didn't miss her as they had never been close, she was her daddy's girl after all. Dennis had given his daughter a lovely wedding before she left, although it was obvious to Cheryl that everyone at the ceremony thought the mother had outshone the bride.

Cheryl had gone to New York to choose her dress, a red one that hugged her figure and was low cut to show off her bubbies; short to show her wonderful legs. It was a great week; she made sure of it by taking "Abs" with her. When he realised he'd left his money at home she'd had to pay for everything but he'd sworn he would pay her back. Come to think of it, he still hadn't. Oh well, she knew he was crazy about her; didn't he show her time and again. He was very young but mature for his age and told her he much preferred older women; said they were much more interesting. Cheryl knew she had the figure of a teenager and worked hard to keep it that way; jogging, working out and living on salads and fruit. She ran her hands lovingly over her body again.

Oh Lord, now she could hear the voice of her neighbour talking to Dennis. Old busy body Marva, always poking her nose in. Probably handing one of her home made macaroni pies to Dennis over the fence. "That means we'll be stuck with that barrel of lard over breakfast." Cheryl spoke aloud. Marva and Cheryl had been school chums but Marva had worn badly and looked much older. She was huge, cooking all those good old West Indian dishes designed to add flab, and boy was she flabby. Her husband had died a few years ago and Dennis did the odd job or two for her around the house while she plied him with fattening food as a thank you. Cheryl would give it to the dogs when she got up; she didn't want to be tempted by all those calories. Better still, she would make Dennis do it. That was always more fun because he felt so guilty; Marva was, in his words, "such a gentle woman who only wants to help." Two of a kind they were, weak and stupid. Their only purpose in life, to be used by people like Cheryl, the winners of the world.

She stretched again, catlike. Where was her breakfast anyway? Just because he had a little work to do was no excuse for being late with her tray. Cheryl got out of bed and walked naked to the window where she studied her husband from behind the curtain. She giggled. He had a massive plaster on his head where she'd hit him last night. What a wimp! His bald head was shining with sweat, fat belly hanging over his shorts which looked massive on his spindly little legs. What a sight for sore eyes! She would certainly make him shower before he brought her breakfast. She could see the plaster on his head glinting in the sunlight, the shape of a white cross. It wasn't the first time she'd struck him but it was always when she'd been drinking that her temper got the better of her; she should really try to cut down on the booze. What a fool he was though; you couldn't help giggling; he looked so funny.

Wait! What was happening now? Marva was in the garden with him. Cheryl thought she must be imagining things. Marva had started to dance round and round on the grass. She was pulling her dress off! Now she was in just her bra and pants! She was taking those off too and Dennis had stopped digging and was going over to her. He was taking off his shorts! What the hell was going on? Dennis was holding the hose pipe over their heads, water was cascading over them. They were kissing!

Right we'll soon see about this! "You'll wish you'd never been born you bastards!" Cheryl cried from the window before turning and running down stairs so fast her feet hardly seemed to touch the ground. She was out in the garden screaming obscenities at them all the way through the red mist that enveloped her. Strangely they took no notice; it was as though she didn't exist. She stopped in front of them, looked around for a weapon. The spade? Then her gaze found the hole Dennis had been digging; there was something in it. She was curious now and moved closer. Then she saw the body. Her body, staring up with sightless eyes. Heaven really couldn't wait!

The cricket ball thumped hard into the sole of my foot, rudely waking me from a strange dream. How much of the match had I missed? Dennis, fielding now, his sweat-drenched head beginning to make the plaster curl off, ran over to retrieve the ball, grinning and apologising as I sat rubbing the pain.

"Sorry but that one got away from me. My back's complainin' wid all de gardening I been doin'. You know how it is don't you?" He was looking at me, still smiling, then he winked and ran back. I felt weird. Could I have a touch of sun stroke?

After the match, my new pals and I headed for the coast road and parked the moke at Oistins fish market. Soon we were tucking into the most delicious fish we had ever eaten, Flying Fish. We washed the meal down with several glasses of dark Bajan rum and coke and by the time we drove slowly back to the hotel, my encounter with the cricketer was forgotten. We strolled across the beach and sat on the sand, looking at the sky which was shot through with red from the setting sun. We talked animatedly of how great life was in Barbados; the easy pace; easy going happy people; wearing shorts all the time. Then there was the swimming, sunbathing, drinking, more drinking and generally having fun. We spoke about ventures we could get into to earn some money so that we could stay on the island and that night under the stars, four inebriated young men full of passion made and lost fortunes, moved into mansions where we held nightly parties with the most beautiful half naked girls in attendance and had Ferraris and Lambourghinis in the garage. We sat in silent contemplation of our sudden wealth and notoriety for some time, before someone suggested sobering ourselves up a little with a moonlit dip. We towelled off afterwards and yes you've guessed it, headed for the bar.

Mark stopped shaking another of his famous cocktails long enough to give me a note which had been left for me. It was from Cecily Ward, the lady I had met at the airport. It was an invitation to a party the following evening. Cecily lived with her family in Atlantic Shores and she had included a little map showing how to get there. What a nice woman.

I hadn't believed for a minute that she would really get in touch with me. After all people were always promising things they had no intention of doing. Maybe Barbadians were different. That night I struck lucky; Monica from Newcastle made it glaringly obvious that she fancied me and I ended up in her room. I would tell you all the details but if someone found my journal I could be arrested! Suffice it to say, if Monica is typical of English girls abroad, no wonder they're so popular.

The following morning, after a jog along the beach followed by a long swim and a large breakfast, I was raring to go again. The first thing I did was hire my own moke. Then I booked scuba diving lessons for the following day before heading off into Bridgetown. At least they drove on the same side of the road as England but this seemed little help when I found myself thrown into the teeming crowds and traffic which jammed the capital. I drove over a stretch of water called the Careenage via a beautiful little bridge which I learned later was called The Chamberlain Bridge. I was glad that the traffic was nose to tail; it gave me the chance to look at the catamarans and yachts and the sidewalk cafes.

I determined to park the moke and walk back to one of them later for a drink. Before the traffic moved again, a stall holder approached offering a piece of her cleverly carved pineapple to sample. She had a little monkey on her shoulder dressed in trousers and waistcoat, with a little fez perched on top of his head, and he hopped onto the seat next to me. What a salesman the little fellow was. Of course I bought a pineapple and some mangoes before driving away. I managed to park the car right next to The Careenage, near a heliport and decided instantly to book a trip over the island.

While I waited I sat looking out over the water, sipping a beer and couldn't believe how at home I felt here since my arrival. Maybe it was the friendliness of the people, the beauty of the island, the fact that it was my first trip abroad or even that I was free of responsibilities for the first time in my life. Perhaps it was all of those things. Yet something strange pulled at me that I couldn't quite put my finger on. I had to smile at myself. Just maybe I was a silly sod who had fallen for the romance of a tropical island like so many tourists did. The helicopter ride was ready.

As we lifted off, I saw a girl struggling to control her wind swept skirt with one hand while keeping her hat clamped to her head with the other. Then she sat down on the harbour wall. Suddenly my stomach was doing a double back flip as we rose fast and I was pre-occupied with enjoying the exhilaration of my first helicopter ride. The pilot had immediately veered left and soon we were flying over a cliff top hotel. with a huge expanse of white sand curving away beneath. This evidently was Crane Beach. Then we were over Sam Lords Castle. I was cross with myself for forgetting to bring my note book with me. Trying to log everything the pilot was saying into my memory proved hopeless. The wild seas of the deserted east coast came up next and the beaches looked magnificent. Then we were over North Point and flying back along the west coast, calm and placid with its little coves. I found each coastline so different and equally fascinating. How long would it take me to explore this lovely country? Trouble was my cash was leaking like a sieve already. I decided that I would book out of the hotel, at the end of the ten day package deal, and in the meantime would find a small flat to rent and would eke out my money for as long as possible.

Back in Bridgetown I went immediately to Cave Shepherd

where I bought three pairs of shorts, some tee shirts and sandals. Then I bought a large sketch pad and several more note books that I would use, not only to record the locations on my travels but also my impressions, and maybe, do a few sketches along the way. In the art section I bought pencils, charcoals, erasers and some pastels, then clutching my carrier bags, I crossed Broad Street and made my way to a cafe beside The Careenage. Here I happily sipped rum while examining my purchases, then sat back to watch the boats, rocking gently in front of me. Such perfect contentment had never been mine before. As I sat, poetry began to form in my mind. Whoa! Moi? Poetry? Bloody pretentious Duncan! But so bloody what! What on earth was happening to me?

On my way back to the car park I saw the old man cycling towards me. Today the dapper fellow was wearing an apple green suit. There was a walking stick strapped to the bike and his curved pipe stuck out of his suit pocket. Once again he tipped his hat to me and I awkwardly raised all my parcels in a return greeting. I wondered just how old he was and made a mental note to ask someone about him.

That evening, despite following the map and getting lost twice, I found myself in Atlantic Shores where lights and loud music pointed the way to Cecily's house. An elderly lady in a battered hat opened the door to me, bowing her head and saying over and over again, "Come in. Yes please. Come in. Come in." Many guests were there already and more were arriving by the minute. Cecily introduced me to her husband and their two grown up boys, who pointed me in the direction of the bar and barbecue, where mouth watering food was in abundance, and the weight of bottles threatened the table legs. Everybody was very friendly, wanting to hear all about me, and I was soon swamped with invitations to their homes.

The rum punches tasted sweet and innocuous and as I finished one, another was placed in my hand. The noise grew. Everybody talked, gossiped, argued politics and religion. Two Trinidadian

sisters were holding onto my arms by now, flirting with me outrageously, laughing and telling me all sorts of stories. When they said that a very famous politician had actually died on the box, I said, "What, on television, in front of all those people?"
There was a stunned silence for a minute, then everybody laughed at once and the sisters explained to me that the politician was having sex with his mistress at the time. I felt really stupid.

Soon after this I collapsed onto the settee feeling very drunk. The party noises continued outside while my head was spinning and heavy, too heavy to lift from the cushion when I became aware of a pair of knowing old eyes studying me. Cecily had introduced me to her maid, the old lady who had invited me in on my arrival and it was she who had cooked all the wonderful food and cleared away. Apparently she had worked for Cecily's mother before her, so was obviously quite an age. She sat on the stairs opposite me now still in her hat, waiting patiently for her glass of rum which eventually arrived. It was a very large glass of rum. She drank some, then sat staring. Cecily had told me that the woman's name was St. Hill. I gave up trying to raise my head and make conversation as I realised, even through my alcoholic haze, that she was totally lost in a world of her own, staring into the depths of the glass.

ODE TO ST. HILL

St. Hill, St. Hill, so old, so still,
Invites you in with toothless grin
Invites you in and invites you in.

St. Hill, St. Hill, toiled all her life,
Child of strife to working wife,
Child of strife to working wife.

St. Hill, St. Hill, you don't complain,
Back so bent from cutting cane,
From cutting cane, cutting cane.

St. Hill, St. Hill, became a maid,
Cleaned and cooked just like a slave,
Like a slave, just like a slave.

St. Hill. St. Hill, so frail and ill,
Skin like my old mahogany tree,
Just like my tree, just like my tree.

St. Hill, St. Hill, sits on the sill,
Waits for the rum to take her fill,
She takes her fill, takes her fill.

St. Hill, St. Hill, eyes in a trance,
Stares into the glass, sees a young girl dance,
Sees a young girl dance, and dance and dance.

WIND SURFING
AT ATLANTIC SHORES

When I awoke the following morning on Cecily's settee, my mouth felt like a parrot's cage. Cecily's two boys appeared out of the kitchen with a jug of water and some freshly squeezed orange juice which they handed me. Afterwards they made me eat some pancakes with maple syrup which I was convinced would make me throw up, but in fact, made me feel much better. The lads said that nobody would be awake for ages, so I might as well go wind surfing with them. They hushed my protests and assured me that they were great teachers and that anyway a salt bath would revive me. I went outside, and looked over the roof tops, of the other houses on Atlantic Shores, to the choppy south coast seas, where the multi-coloured sails of wind surfers already dotted the horizon. Excitement filled me and suddenly I was sober again and ready to go.

What a day it turned out to be. Under the boy's tuition, I stood up, balanced for a while, then fell in so many times I lost count. I did it until my legs turned to jelly, then I rested, had a drink and carried on. When I eventually got the hang of it, the exhilaration was something else. Never have I felt anything like it! Flying over the waves, driven by the wind and free as a bird, as one with the elements and somehow more aware of everything around me. Truly out of this world. On the way back home to Cecily's, we picked up Chinese take-aways and sat watching *The Bold And The*

Beautiful on television while we ate. The episode had been filmed in Barbados.

When I finally returned that night to the hotel and told them all I could wind surf, I expected everyone to be impressed and was surprised when they started snickering. Then I looked in the mirrors, behind the bar, and half a dozen white eyed Duncans stared back at me, out of a face the colour of a freshly boiled lobster. Suddenly I was in agony. Mark picked several aloe leaves from the garden and told me to smother myself with the sap and take some Aspirin. The aloe was smelly but incredibly cooling and after gently easing myself onto the bed, I finally managed to sleep for a few hours.

The next day, after liberally coating myself once more with aloe, covering it with factor thirty and climbing gingerly into loose cotton trousers and a long sleeved shirt, I stuck my base ball cap on my head and gingerly faced the world again. Today I would keep totally out of the sun. I had been told that there were many fine artists and art galleries on the island, which sounded like the perfect way to spend a day in the shade. Perhaps some of them even had air conditioning. I telephoned the scuba club and put off my lessons for a few days.

According to my little tourist guide book, the Kirby Gallery was nearest, so I put the hood up on the moke and was there in five minutes. Oh heaven, as I opened the gallery door, cool air hit me. Inside I found an eclectic array of wonderfully vivid artwork and stared entranced at the soft curves and beautiful blue lit faces of Bosco Holder's women, oozing sexuality and gazed in awe at portraits of Marilyn Monroe from the brush of Patrick Foster together with his lavender fantasy pastels. I found that I just couldn't leave several works of the Careenage by Wayne Branch whose water begged me to dip my fingers in. If only I had the money to buy some of these. I could always rob the bank where I used to work of course but better still, I should learn to paint like these artists! Oh there was so much to do. The lady at the desk

advised me to drive out to a village near the Four Square rum factory, which housed many shops and an excellent art gallery with a particularly interesting exhibition showing for the next few weeks.

On my way to the village, I was about to pass The Champagne Bar but decided it looked too inviting to miss. It was right on the sea which was rough and the salt breezes whipped my clothes, cooling my burning skin and spraying salt over the moke when I parked. I chose a seat opposite the bar on a small table for two, directly overlooking the sea. White gossamer curtains hung from the ceiling to the floor and billowed their response to the wind, stroking my cheek softly from time to time. Without turning my head I could study the people around me. I sipped champagne as I waited for the lobster salad I had ordered to arrive and wondered how much this little extravagance was going to deplete the coffers but then I could have sworn I heard mum say, "Have one for me Duncan!" and couldn't help smiling.

I could overhear an interesting group of extremely arty looking types talking loudly, gesticulating extravagantly with every word. Into this gathering glided a vision of old world loveliness. Everything she wore, from a large picture hat to ornate court shoes and long dangly earrings, were lilac through lavender to brilliant violet. Her long flowing chiffon dress moved around her in perfect partnership with the curtains and the sea, so that she appeared to vibrate in her gossamer loveliness. A long flimsy scarf was bound once round her neck and the ends fell to the hem of her dress. She was heavily made up, blue eye shadow, false eye lashes and a red gash for a mouth; she was like something from a twenties movie. There were shrieks as the group caught sight of her.

"Margot darling, where have you been?" Everyone moved round to make a space for her next to them. She flung her hat onto the table, which made each of them lunge forward to save their drinks, and settled herself between two young good looking men. "Champagne all round sweetie!" she called to the bar man; then listened quietly while a dozen questions were fired at her. Finally, champagne flutes filled and toasts completed, Margot spoke.

FINE ART

My children, I have a strange, uncanny tale to tell. Do not utter a word until I am finished! I shall set the scene. The group, in unison, eagerly leaned forward.

It was one of those typical balmy West Indian nights darlings, you know the sort of thing; stars scattered on the night sky like a million diamonds, sound of waves lapping on sandy beaches, the air thick with the smell of frangipanni, ladies of the night and best of all darlings, us! Our little group consisted of artistes variosos; painters, sculptors, poets, writers, actors (strictly legit theatre darlings) and singers (classical naturally). All banded together, much as we are now, talking nineteen to the dozen and more often than not, all at once; putting the world to rights while consuming vast quantities of wine and generally looking quite lovely in our flowing white island cottons. Behind the closed doors of our inner sanctum of intellectual superiority, we decided to call ourselves the Hip Hedonists of Hastings, or the Three H Club. Why Hastings darlings? Well simply because we always gathered at Peter's studio in that district. Margot took a cigarette which she pushed into the longest cigarette holder I had ever seen, while half a dozen lighters pushed forward for the honour of lighting it for her. She inhaled deeply and they all waited in silence as the smoke billowed out of her nostrils. Then she spoke again.

We were all standing neck deep in our usual cacophony of chatter in Peter's huge studio, admiring his latest works, when he silenced everyone, as he does. Margot paused and looked around for approbation from the others, which she received, then she continued. Peter stood, arms outstretched, head bowed, waiting quite properly for the full dramatic pause in which one could hear the proverbial pin drop, darlings. When all was quiet, he finally unveiled his wonderful ideas to launch our club (which incidentally would coincide with the launch of his latest works, dears, but you know Peter, always the one to spot an advantage and spear it before anyone else does). Hey ho. Anyway, he told us that his next exhibition would be a show to transcend all others and that he wanted our individual expertise to combine and bring to fruition his phenomenal vision.

Well sweeties, you can imagine the effect. Ideas erupted like larva flow from Mount Vesuvius. Trouble with us artistes, darlings, is we don't just think we're right all the time, we all know it as an absolute certainty. Giggles burst from the group before Margot silenced them with a glance. Therefore we clash interminably with roars, thunder, tears and pouts but things usually get sorted out in the end. Well dears, the planning, talking, designing went on all night and didn't stop for the next two months. Finally, the show to end all shows; *l'exposition extraordinaire et incroyable*, my sweets was organised. We were ready.

We chose the village alongside the Four Square rum distillery. It was the perfect venue with its interesting paving and gardens, pretty vendors' carts and most important, the lovely art gallery and sunken open air theatre. Altogether quite divine darlings and just made for the Three H Club venture. So this is where we decided to hold the 'Happening' as we all began to call it. This would consist of the paintings naturally, which would be displayed in the gallery; drama, poetry, music and dance in the theatre. These, the finest talents from the world d'art my angels, we would season with mysticism, love, hallucinogens, sixties flower power, all that stuff darlings. Invitations to a select few were sent out; ambassadors, diplomats, professional people, government ministers, members of the plantocracy. Had to include a few of the filthy rich from the west coast, not that one really wanted them of course but quite honestly, darlings, they are the only bloody people who ever buy anything–if the frame is big enough that is! There were shrieks of laughter. Margot smiled before continuing.

Show evening arrived. The event was called *Nirvana–A Journey Through The Senses*. The ensemble of guests gathered together that evening outside the gallery. Simon, the cordon blue chef of our group, had arranged Three H Club gods and goddesses to serve his special cocktails which he called Nectars from flower bedecked vendor carts. What was in the Nectars? One didn't ask darlings. God only knows the concoction but more than two and we were walking with Olympians! The food, oh darlings, the food was exquisite. Very simple, a delicate finger buffet of melt-in-the-mouth manna prepared by angels. My task had been twofold; one, to write a little piece about the event which we presented to the guests on a scroll tied with white ribbon and two, give a welcoming speech to set the scene.

As the guests entered the gallery I began. The first thing I did was to assure them all, that they were in for an evening to transcend all others. I said, "The Gods themselves will look down from Mount Olympus and feel their senses titillated by the scene unfolding before them. Unbelievable beauty to fill the eyes, heavenly notes to charm the ears and divine delicacies to send taste buds into an orgasm of delight; providing an ethereal evening of magic and drama. On our palette is an art gourmet's medley of self indulgence."

Inside the gallery the audience gasped at Peter's work. They were spellbound as I spoke to them.
"Peter's canvasses exude sensuality, he pays true homage to the vulnerability of the naked form with awesome skin tones and a light that radiates and fills one with the gentle warmth of early morning sun, leaving a tingle of well-being and a strange desire to follow one's loins wherever they may lead."
Margot looked around. They loved that bit.

"His work speaks with hot breath, whispering: This is how it should be. In a world so full of wonders, our allotted time is too short by far, so it is necessary to fill life's cup to the brim. Enjoyment is the essence darlings."

I couldn't help noticing how many hands held each other, how many smouldering looks passed between liquid eyes, fingers that brushed as if by chance against straining breasts and I don't think it was entirely due to our Fairy Fly Cakes. I continued.

"Having given birth to his creation, the artist must endure a traumatic separation when his child is sold and becomes another's. Chameleon-like the paintings become, like it or not, the dreams and interpretations of the new owner. Therefore, categorising each one becomes a lesson in futility. Instead let each painting become a stage and let us, the audience, be the directors."

At this point my listeners became visibly even more excited, whether the sheer beauty before them, the drinks, the heavy scent on the night air, or the stars that were so big they seemed to be pressing against the windows to come in, I don't know. In any event, they all really entered into the spirit of The Happening and directed each dramatic canvas with great imagination.

'As we gaze at the canvas, the artist unfolds for us an Othello of high drama. But wait! Stage left, the sorcerer's apprentice blends a magic brew; another scene and the soulful voice of Ella fills the air and we are lifted to the high plane of pure spirit. Or sent to a secret meditative rendezvous where just as one is relaxing, a chuckle builds out of nowhere and realisation comes that the throat is yours.' Walcott's words come, "I have felt the beads in my blood erupt as my brush stroked their backs."

I ended my recitation as follows: "The paintings are earth and sky, spirit, love and departure; dreams, reflections, music, poetry, drama and life. In some respects, I share this introspective with you, urging the thought that Peter's art should be viewed through rose-coloured nipples. A girl called Marilyn once said, 'I'm not interested in money, I just want to be wonderful.' Well, ladies and gentlemen, this Happening is just that. Oscar Wilde thought the secret of life is art, so let Peter take us by the hand in pursuit of that secret and let us all be wonderful!"

We all followed Peter's lead, skipping and frolicking behind him along the paved pathways and into the theatre, the low murmurings from his, by now strangely mesmerised but vocal audience building to a rumble with crickets and tree frogs in chorus. Fireflies filled the night and settled like fairies in the trees to sit, listen and watch.

As everyone arrived at the theatre, each person was handed a heavily scented bloom and perfume filled the air from strategically placed vases holding jasmine and tuber roses. More delicacies and Nectars were passed on silver trays by lovely hedonists in flimsy Greek tunics while an introductory poem was read that brought the guests to new heights. Ballerinas danced on air with gossamer wings and filled our souls with longing while voices rose so sweetly that water came to our eyes. Music brought us to a tranquillity and meditation that was sublime. Mantras were artfully hidden in repeating phrases while mandalas were played about the walls from camouflaged projectors. Simulated sex acts were performed in time honoured Greek fashion but then it seemed to spread to the audience darlings! Coupling seemed to be happening everywhere but it all seemed so normal nobody took any notice. Truly all of us were in heaven, a combined consciousness propelled to a Nirvana so fantastic that the gods themselves must have looked down in envy, wanting to share our joy. We all said as much darlings. The feasting, in every sense of the word my loves, went on into the night. We called to the gods to join us! Oh my dears, you should have been there. Margot looked wistful; she suddenly seemed to sober; her head bent and fingers wrenched at the chiffon scarf hanging from her neck and dropped it into her lap. Her rapt audience waited expectantly.

And that darlings is the crux of the problem. There we were, all one hundred of us plus the Hip Hedonists from Hastings Club. Well I say, there we were but that's where the trouble lies.

Suddenly we didn't know where we were exactly. We were moving away from the ground, as though being pulled by a huge magnet. Soon we were very high, so high in fact we could see the village and the theatre below us. The odd cloud was passing, not above us but through us. And still we were rising. The thought occurred to some of us that perhaps we had made too many references to gods and heaven and had upset someone somewhere. Others said that was tosh. That we were so very lovely and talented that we were all meant for higher things. Who knows darlings? Anyway the Club didn't seem too bothered; they were far too busy arguing about which parish we were passing over.

We all agreed when one of the Hedonists said, "One does have to wonder, darling, what will happen to Barbados without all our beauty and talent and the combined power of all these important people?" At that, there was such a strange noise, growing louder by the minute.

"Good grief!" we cried in unison as the entire land beneath us began shaking! Shaking my darlings with, well it sounded for all the world like, an awfully loud chuckle!

The group around Margot all started talking at once, arguing loudly about the meaning of such a story. Margot got up, pushed another cigarette into the holder, retrieved her hat and said, "Darlings I must fly." But by this time, the discussion was hot and they didn't notice Margot leave. They complained later that typically, she hadn't settled her bill first.

I had seen her leave, if you can call it that. She looked straight at me and gave me a winsome smile as she stood up. Her flowing robes appeared to tangle, roll and curl with the billowy curtains and when they unfurled, she was gone! I shook my head, tried to make myself believe I had imagined it but I knew it was all true.

I left the Champagne Bar feeling very odd and on my way to the Four Square village, had great difficulty coming to terms with what I had witnessed. I felt strangely detached from it all, separated from reality somehow. Immediately I arrived, I felt that I had been there before; obviously Margot had painted the scene well. Sure enough there was a really unusual exhibition in the gallery but somehow I couldn't get into it, couldn't focus my attention. My thoughts kept returning to Margot, her Three H Club and their *"exhibition extraordinaire et incroyable"*, especially when I wandered around the pretty streets and stepped down into the sunken theatre. At first I thought I heard music and laughter but when I looked around there was nobody about. Suddenly my senses literally reeled with the heady aroma of scented blossoms and then I saw them. The images were human in form but gossamer, appearing and disappearing like wispy clouds caught in whirling eddies; they wore togas and danced in the strong sunlight. They came right up to me, laughing faces, inviting me to join in and I, cowardly foolish creature that I am, hid my face in my hands and when I looked up, they had gone. I felt that I had been offered something vital, something wonderful, life altering. An essence in me had been recognised and a door was opened; all I had to do was walk through.

I drove back to the hotel quite subdued and by the time I arrived, had convinced myself that the previous day's sunburn must have addled my brain. The group I had travelled out with were going home the next day but I slipped away from the farewell party early, too aware that my melancholy was showing and not wanting to spoil their fun. I had an early night and slept like a log.

The next day I went to the airport to see my friends off to England and we all agreed that we'd never known time pass so quickly. They said they all envied me and wished they could be staying on. Monica got quite tearful. I don't know why because we'd only had that one session together, after that it became apparent that I was only one on a list of ten (one for each day) she was ticking off. But we'd become good pals and promised to write. Even so, actually saying good bye was tough and I felt quite home sick for a while especially when they started talking about England, the Saturday football match and their girl friends. I watched the plane's lights fade into the night sky while standing on top of a grassy knoll beside the airport, then I headed back to the hotel to pick up my things. I was moving into my flat and I was like a kid with a new toy.

My apartment in Navy Gardens, was still only a short walk away from Accra beach and I was thrilled with it. There were steps leading up to a good size balcony where I could entertain all the friends whose hospitality I had been receiving; there were two bedrooms, a decent size lounge, kitchen and bathroom. It was well furnished and spotlessly clean. The one slight problem was that the wall between the kitchen and bathroom didn't go right up to the ceiling, so any noises made in the bathroom could easily be heard in the rest of the apartment. Never mind, I would just have to remember to play the music louder when I had guests. Tonight I would have a house warming party.

The next day I was in great spirits. The house warming had gone really well, everybody enjoyed themselves and were quite impressed with my new pad. I had taken it easy with the booze as it was my diving class and I refused to let anything spoil that. Scuba diving, I discovered, was without doubt the best, most exciting thing I had ever done. From that first day, getting all the gear on and going to the bottom of the swimming pool where our instructor, Andy, taught us the essential sign language and where we got used to the heavy tanks, I had loved diving with a passion. We graduated to the shallows of the sea the following day and when we went out to the coral at last, it was unbelievable. My lessons had opened up a new world to me and all the time I was learning I could think of nothing else. Imagine the euphoria when, having completed the diving course, I was certified PADI. I felt ridiculously pleased with myself.

Andy, to celebrate the end of his courses, always offered a day trip to the Tobago Cays where he said the diving was incredible. It was expensive but I consoled myself with the fact that I'd moved into the flat so would save a lot of money on hotel bills. I grabbed my passport and money, feeling a real thrill when I locked my own door and made my way to the beach. The bus was waiting there and most of my friends from the diving school were already on board. We would over night in Bequia so that we could enjoy the following day on the reefs, then back to Barbados that night.

The flight was delayed, which our instructor said was normal, so we waited quite happily in the Voyager Lounge. After a couple of rum and cokes which hit my empty stomach like a bomb, I decided to eat something. Everything looked delicious but I soon settled on some macaroni cheese pie, two flying fish and a ladle full of beef stew on top. It was wonderful. My friends were still up at the bar and I watched them swilling back the rum as I ate. No way would I risk feeling hung over for the diving tomorrow. As I ate I couldn't help overhearing the conversation between two middle aged ladies at the table next to mine. One seemed to be persuading her friend Mo, not to fly off to Canada.

MO'S NEW EYES

Mo said her vision was not much cop
And was off to Canada for a laser op.
The friends sat at Grantley waiting for the plane,
And spoke of life, what they lose and gain.

Kay said, "God saw us getting old and frail
And fixed it so our eyes would fail.
A sort of built in rose coloured specs
So we won't notice we're becoming wrecks.

Mo, when the doc's repaired your eyes,
Prepare yourself for a big surprise.
You'll see my face is looking baggy,
My rear end drooped and kinda saggy.
So if you want my friendship evermore
Pretend I look just as before.

Ignore the lines around my eyes,
The cellulite that hugs my thighs.
Cross two fingers on your right hand,
Smile and say, "Kay, you're looking grand."
As though we haven't enough to bear,
Dolly birds, big boobs and long blond hair.
Why can't our vision be more like men's,
Who, as wives age, can't comprehend
That while we crumble, crease and bore,
They stay handsome! Sex appeal galore!

Mo pondered this and began to smile,
Crow's feet crinkled, mouth stretched a mile.
"You're right. I feel good! I look good too!
Sod the op. Kay, I'm coming home with you."

will always remember my trip to the Tobago Cays. The diving gear was provided and we were soon heading out to sea in three small boats. When I tumbled off and the water flowed over me, I felt I had entered another world. Beautiful living multi coloured coral structures of massive proportions opened up before me while avenues of sand invited me to explore the marine wonderland. Everything was crystal clear; I could see for miles; the bright sun twinkled down and sparkled through the water around me. Many of the fish were like those I'd grown used to in Barbados, Parrot Fish, Damsel, Angel and Trumpet Fish but were twice the size. There were many more varieties that I hadn't seen before. Suddenly a group of squid appeared from nowhere and made a circle around me, staring as though attempting a silent communion. Then the weird and wonderful Puffa Fish swam up, and then shyly backed away again, and it maddened me to think how such beautiful creatures were caught and sold to tourists for lamp shades. The beauty of the Cays affected all of us and we were sad, when the time came, to bid a reluctant farewell to beautiful Bequia and its people but we all promised to go back one day.

On the short flight back to Barbados, I sat in front of a woman who looked so much like Mo, the lady who had been going to get her eyes fixed, that I thought they must be sisters. She was telling her companion how worried she was that she kept forgetting things and thought she might be losing her mind. The man seemed to be concerned and gave her the address of a good doctor in Bridgetown.

PRESCRIPTION FOR MRS. C.

You say that you are fretting,
You're confused and it's upsetting,
Over things you keep forgetting Mrs. C.?
Just relax Mrs. C.
Let's have the facts Mrs. C?

To encounter your grey matter,
You must first remove your hat, eh?
Lie right here, next to me Mrs. C.
You have my ear Mrs. C.
Loud and clear now Mrs. C.

By your fears you are pursued?
Your fantasies are always crude?
You dream of frolics in the nude Mrs. C.?
No, that's not rude Mrs. C.
Don't be a prude Mrs. C.

But we must relieve your tension,
Bring you to a new dimension,
There's a method I could mention Mrs. C.
Though not related Mrs. C.
Let's get naked Mrs. C.

I don't believe in pills or potions,
If I just increase these motions,
Massage you with this lotion Mrs. C.
Let go, just sink Mrs. C.
I'm on the brink Mrs. C.

Your mind will stop its churning
As your memory starts returning,
From such experiments we are learning Mrs. C,
Go with the flow Mrs. C
Is that your toe Mrs. C.?

What! Your memory has come back?
I'm not a doctor, I'm a quack?
You will ensure I get the sack Mrs. C.?
It's true, I'm no M.D. Mrs. C.
But you came to me Mrs. C.

The doctor's in the other street.
I'm your butcher. Here's your meat.
You're in shock! Please take a seat Mrs. C.
Meat's good for the brain Mrs. C.
Please come again Mrs. C.

The days were running into weeks and since my move to the flat all my pals, mostly locals, seemed to congregate at my place every evening. Then it was off to one of the clubs or bars. Sometimes I feel that I have lost the purpose of my journey. I am getting fed up with it. Half the time I can't remember where we've been, and the other half I seemed to spend throwing up. Looking into the mirror this morning, a drunk with dark circles under his eyes who looked ten years older stared back. I was determined to break free of my boozy companions for a couple of days, and in so doing, return my blood to something under eighty per cent proof. I showered, shaved and dressed; picked up my map and got into the moke. Today would be different. First I would drive into Bridgetown and get some breakfast.

Crossing over the bridge I passed my regal old man again. He was wheeling his bike and had the pipe in his mouth; his suit was bright orange. I would have liked to stop and talk to him but the traffic was pressing me forward. Instead I shouted, "Hello!" and waved. The old man raised his pipe and walked slowly on.

Over breakfast I decided to visit Farley Hill where the film *Island In The Sun* with Harry Bellafonte had been shot. I had vague recollections of my mother singing a song from the movie. Nearby apparently there was a monkey sanctuary where the animals roamed free; I would really like to see that. Walking back to the car park I saw four dogs following a bag lady. I slowed my pace and watched as she settled herself into a shop doorway and started repairing the holes in her shoes with newspaper. As the dogs lay down beside her, I felt myself strangely moved by the scene. Tentatively (because I thought she might be offended) I crossed over the road and stopping beside her, gave her a twenty dollar note. She hadn't asked for anything which made me feel humble but she accepted the gift with a lovely smile.

THAT'S LIFE

Kaylene called to Patch, Bandit, Jake and Diamond; they were finishing feeding off the catch that had escaped the fishermen's nets. The fish lay, mouths agape, as though calling to her dogs, "Breakfast is ready, come and get it!" Hee, hee, that's life! She heard herself chuckling and that made her laugh more until she caught the expressions on the faces of the passers-by and made herself stop. Oh, but the view across Carlisle Bay was beautiful, colours in the sea that made your heart glad. You could feel God walking beside you.

Her eyes were very bad now. One time she was sure she'd had spectacles but she couldn't remember what had happened to them. Kaylene forgot so much these days but that's life! Old age didn't come alone. Funny though, inside she still felt young, like a girl and could remember things from when she was young real well.

She stopped for a minute to wipe the perspiration from her face and neck with a piece of old cloth she carried. Man, it was hot already and the sun still not overhead. Her animals looked up as if to say "All right Kaylene? Can we go on now?" Hee, hee. She pulled up her skirt and tightened the string that held it close round her waist, noticing the toes poking out of her shoes, and made a mental note to repair them later with newspaper. She picked her way slowly on down Bay Street and then the Chamberlain Bridge came into view over the Careenage. This was her favourite spot and she stopped a while to drink in the sight, finally moving on towards a café.

The white lady who owned the café was nice and greeted her

with a smile and a bag that Kaylene knew contained some breakfast for her; sugared rolls, a paw paw maybe and a plastic cup with a lid that would hold sweet coffee. Sometimes she slipped yesterday's newspaper in too; Kaylene loved a good read. The lady bade her move on quickly. Hee hee, move quickly? Not any more. Once upon a time she moved real fast man, she could move her hips wham, wham – make all the fellas' tongues loll out! Sure they did! She was De Wildey Wuk Up Queen. None better. True though! Kaylene thought back, chupsed and chuckled again. Child, the stories I could tell; make your toes curl! All so long ago. But that's life child.

She peered at the deep sea fishing boats and the fancy yachts that lined the Careenage as she passed. Somewhere deep in her memory she vaguely recalled being at sea under the stars with her Trevor. Remembered the feel of hard muscles, mouth sucking at her breasts and a hot tongue; the wind cold on her sweaty body. People were looking again and Kaylene realised she was rubbing at her lower belly. Hee, hee. Off she went over the bridge stopping to play with the monkey at the fruit seller's stall but the woman shooshed her on.

Kaylene passed by the boat that was a bar, full of tourists who called to her and waved. One shouted, "Darlin' come and have a drink. What are you doin' tonight love? Comin' dancin' with me?" Hee, hee, they were nice enough young fellas but she had always preferred her men dark. She wondered briefly though what a white man would be like, could he 'stand pon it long' like her Trevor. Ooh that man was so bad he was good. The best! For a moment she felt lonely for him and wondered where he could be but then looked down at her canine quartet and smiled; they all really loved each other.

As they reached the traffic lights, Bandit took the lead and she followed behind Diamond, Jake and Patch across the road past Mannings where she looked upwards to the Norman Centre and her dim eyes could just make out the ladies standing way up in their

fancy dresses, unmoving. She shook her head and sighed, then moved the strange procession on to the next set of lights and crossed over Broad Street. Kaylene always crossed there so she could smell the lovely perfumes as she passed Harrisons. She always stopped to gaze at the tourists in their bright shorts with their red faces and burnt knees. Some stared at her as they went by and she felt like shouting 'What! You rass'ole idiots! You never seen a poor old black lady before?' Hee, hee. But she didn't say anything. Kaylene looked at her own arms shrivelled and blackened like leather from the constant sun, the long hard hours of working, can't see to can't see, in the fields. Funny though, she couldn't actually recall cutting the cane. She sucked at her teeth remembering the sweet taste of cane juice in her mouth and felt the hunger grip her belly; it was time for breakfast. Bandit, Jake, Diamond and Patch were already lying in her doorway at the side of Harrisons and she soon lowered herself down with them, positioning her carrier bags close to her. She watched a young man hovering about on the opposite side of the street; he seemed to be trying to make up his mind about something; then with long strides he was beside her smiling and giving her a twenty dollar bill. Well, what a nice young man. Kaylene thanked him and watched him as he walked away. She got comfortable and wiped the sweat from herself again and eagerly opened her package. Life was good nuh?

She was full and feeling at peace with the world, sipping her coffee and watching the people go by. There was Tall Man with his long trousers with the shorts on top, hand always out for a dollar. He was a quiet one, never even said hello to anybody but then it takes all sorts. He could have troubles. Now that was odd; Moving Man was over there, heading for Swan Street. He mostly roved the countryside and carried what seemed to be a houseful of stuff on his back. What was he doing in the city? She finished her coffee and put everything back in the bag to dispose of one time. She kept Barbados clean, not like some. Kaylene opened her paper just as The Professor called a good morning. She waved back. As always, he had pieces of cloth tied all over him, a large bag over his shoulder and a massive file of papers in his arms. He always looked so busy, intent on being somewhere else.

Kaylene squinted down at the newspaper and found she couldn't read much of the print, but she studied all the pictures. When she was finished with the pages, she began repairing her shoes with them so that her toes would not stick out. The procedure took a while to get right but she had learned from previous harsh experience how uncomfortable it could be walking if you got it wrong. Job done, she rested back contentedly to people watch. Her eyes soon grew heavy as the mesmerising legs trooped by, all different colours and sizes and soon she was sleeping like a baby.

Kaylene awoke with a start! A white face was into hers talking at her. "What de hell she tink she doin? She make I jump!" The woman seemed to be very cross. Kaylene was confused, what had she done to this lady? She sat up and concentrated on trying to understand. The lady called her "Mother" and "Kay" and asked where she had been all these days.

She said, "Mother, we told you before, if you ever run away again we will put you in Black Rock!"
Kaylene began to cry. She didn't know or understand the woman but she did know of Black Rock and didn't want to go there. Could this stranger send her to that place? She asked the lady why she was treating a poor black woman so?
The lady let out a big sigh and sprayed some sweet smelling stuff onto Kaylene's arm and rubbed hard saying, "Look, mother, look. You are a white woman; you live in a big house on the west coast with maids and everything. Oh darling, come on, dry your eyes. We won't really send you to Black Rock. We're just at our wits end for ways to stop you running away from home!"
The lady who seemed to think she was Kaylene's daughter, helped her to her feet as a large car drew up. "Now here's the chauffeur to pick us up mother, we're going home."
To Kaylene's surprise Bandit, Jake, Patch and Diamond jumped

into the back of the big car obviously very at home in it, happy tails wagging. Kaylene followed meekly.

She settled back into the rich leather; it sure smelled good. It was nice and cool as the car moved silently down Broad Street passing the Professor and Tall Man but although she waved they didn't seem to see her at all, at all. They drove past the bus terminal at Fairchild Street, around and back across the Chamberlain Bridge where, because of the traffic, they had to stop by the fruit seller with the monkey and to Kaylene's surprise, the monkey was lifted up for her to pet. She thought to herself how funny it was that when she was a poor black woman, she was treated very differently to now that she was a white woman in a big posh car. But that's life! A handsome young man passed in front of the car and cheekily promised a night of fun. Hee, hee, ooh those muscles! It was funny though, she thought, even though she was now a white woman, she decided she still liked her meat dark! Hee, hee.

The lady who said she was her daughter rapped suddenly with her knuckles on the window separating them from the old chauffeur, 'Get a move on Trevor, we want to get home for cocktails!' In the rearview mirror, Kaylene's eyes locked with Trevor's. He smiled and winked.

Hee, hee. That's life.

I was feeling good, I'd given the bag lady twenty dollars, it was a beautiful breezy day and I was on my way to Farley Hill. Best of all, I was sober for a change. I had decided to keep to the coast road past Brandons Beach, along the Spring Garden Highway to the parish of St James. This was the rich coast; exorbitantly priced hotels, massive beach side houses and golf course homes of the multi-millionaires. One day I would return and explore the hotels buy a beer in every bar, if my money allowed, and mix with the rich people for a while. Maybe some would rub off! I passed by a pretty chattel house village of pastel coloured shops and drove on through Holetown. There were masses of people about and traffic was bumper to bumper. It was the Holetown Festival and interesting stalls lined the roadway while tantalising aromas assailed my nostrils, inviting me to stay and eat. But I was determined to stick to my schedule. Soon I turned right by Porters and at the top of the hill, saw the prettiest little chattel house; it was pink with hooded shutters where frilly white curtains moved in the breeze. I just had to stop and take a photograph. There was no one about so I took a couple of shots. A rocking chair sat outside, and on closer inspection, I found the white curtains were covered in pink flowers and that a previously well tended garden had become scruffy and over grown. The place looked deserted but why leave a delightful little rocking chair behind? Perhaps whoever lived here had rocked his life away on this porch and was now dead? Somehow I didn't think so. I didn't think it was a 'he' who had left this house either. I reluctantly left 'my' little chattel house, vaguely wondering how much it would cost to buy a place like that. I continued on my way, past The Royal Westmoreland Golf Course, and a while later, drove through a village called Mile and a Quarter. I wondered where it was a mile and a quarter from? Or maybe to?

At last in the parish of St. Peter, I saw the sign for Farley Hill and turning into the drive, was directed to where I could park the car. Farley Hill was lovely, cool and shady and I walked slowly towards the imposing ruins where they had filmed *Island In The Sun*. I seemed to have the place to myself. It was quiet, yet the wind pushed its way through the trees and a thousand voices filled the air with whispers. It was not difficult to see elegant ladies and gentlemen from another time appearing and disappearing, dancing around the columns to silent melodies. I walked up a hill, at the top of which were fabulous views of the Scotland district, right across to the distant rugged east coast with its wild seas and incredible beaches. That would be my next trip! Right now I was bound for the Wildlife Reserve which was close by.

After parking the car at the Reserve I strolled into an old signal station near by. A taped recording gave a brief history of the place as I looked at relics left by the soldiers who had served there which were displayed in glass cases. I climbed the stairs and waited until the tape ended and it became quiet so that I could feel the atmosphere. Looking out of the slits in the walls at the views beyond I heard the shouts of the soldiers' voices; my heart thumped in panic with theirs.

"Duncan, lad you'd better get back on the booze, you're seeing more ghosties and ghoulies without it!"

I walked slowly along the road to The Wild Life Reserve. It was so cool and breezy; quiet too with very few people about.

THE BOSCOBELLE BOYS

Harry's mother called him in from play. She wanted him to get some provisions and said that he must take his young brother Tom with him. Harry hated going for provisions, especially when the gang had such a good game going, but what made it worse was that he had to take young Tom along. His little brother was a pain in the neck. Shouts of "Boscobelle!" could be heard coming from his mates calling him back to the game. His father had been born in Boscobelle on the east coast, where his gran and grandad still lived and whom they visited often, so he was always called Boscobelle. Dad had four sons including us, Harry and Tom, all of whom were also called Boscobelle, just like Dad. It was confusing sometimes, like when someone shouted and they all answered at once.

But then Mum, who came originally from another island on a fishing boat, always said with a superior air, "Barbados is a peculiar place. Everyone talks funny."

Harry explained to his friends that he would be back soon and set off with Tom. They decided to cut across Sandy Lane Golf Course because it was much quicker. As the boys came to the seventh tee they stopped, and looked down at the green far below, and Tom asked, as he always did, how the golfers could get their ball all the way down and into the hole where the flag was. Harry had explained a dozen times, in fact every time they came this way, but patiently did so again, that the golfers could take more than one shot to get the ball into the hole. Tom still didn't seem to understand.

The view from their high vantage point on the seventh tee was stunning. Looking out over the course to the glistening Caribbean Sea beyond, Harry's little chest puffed out as he breathed in the beauty of it all. Pointing out to sea, he showed Tom a massive boat called the Queen Elizabeth sailing majestically off into the blue, to far off lands with exotic sounding names.

"They are off to who knows where Tom. One day when we're big, we'll go too!"

"Harry, where's 'who knows where'?"

Thinking of exotic far away places, Harry glanced over to the left where the big wall surrounded the Italian Countess' house. Even though he had Tom with him, he couldn't resist the temptation to go to the secret hole in the wall and spy on the lovely lady. He grabbed his little brother and made him swear not to tell their mother about the secret he was about to share. Tom said that he wasn't allowed to swear. Harry was losing patience.

"If you tell, your ears will go purple!" Harry hissed.
Tom quite liked that idea but wisely didn't voice his opinion, realising that his brother was getting agitated with him. Harry often got agitated.

"You must be quiet as a mouse. She is from a country far away called Italy. Her name is Patricia de... de... oh something or other!"

By this time, they had squeezed behind the bushes and were looking through the hole.

"Is that Patriishdedeosomefingofher?"

"Sshhh. Be quiet Tom, or I shall take you home!"

What luck, the Countess was in the garden with her handsome husband and several important looking people who were all sipping champagne and eating caviar. He could smell the caviar from here. Harry had spied on many of the rich people's parties and he was getting quite knowledgeable about their cuisine. Everything was served on silver platters proffered by circulating maids in little white aprons; there was asparagus, smoked salmon and the smallest pizzas and quiches Harry had ever seen in his life. As the guests chatted, the Countess moved among them. She was wearing a floating green dress that fell to the ground and showed off her eyes bewitchingly. The breeze caught the dress as she passed from guest to guest and it looked to Harry as though she was floating, just like the fairy princess he thought she really was. Harry was a little in love with the Countess, if you hadn't guessed already.

One day he had been at the spy hole when Patricia was all alone in the garden. His heart had come up into his mouth as it seemed she was walking directly over to him and he would surely be discovered. But no. She stopped close enough for him to smell her delightful perfume, then she reached out a hand so white, so delicate with long tapering fingers that he thought he could see right through it. She plucked a lime and bringing it to her nose, inhaled deeply. Her face was serene, skin like porcelain and her blond hair was pulled back, highlighting her perfect features. Ah, he sighed with that first young love that pierces the heart.

"I'm bored." Tom's whines shattered the mood. He was sitting under a palm, picking his nose. "I'm really, really fed up!" Harry clamped a hand over his little brother's mouth to stop his chattering and moved away quickly, clambering over the rocks, down towards the flag fluttering below the seventh tee. When they got to the green, a golf ball was lying invitingly close to the hole. Looking far up to the golfers above, Harry had an idea and screaming at Tom to run, he grabbed the ball and they took off for the bushes across the fairway. When they reached the shelter, they collapsed laughing, watching the fat man jumping up and down waving his club through the air. Harry then lifted the ball high and it landed in the bunker beside the green. What a laugh! This was fun; perhaps Tom wasn't too bad after all and thinking this, Harry decided to take the young'un to watch the bikini clad ladies at Sandy Lane Hotel.

They had guards at the gate. 'Mainly to keep out the hoi poloi', their mother said, so they had to be careful. Scampering from the cover of one tree to another, Tom felt very proud that Harry was at last treating him like a grown up and was determined not to let him down. Tom was very impressed with the fish that darted and swam through the pools beside the steps and when he saw the arch at the entrance to the lobby with the sea beyond, he thought it was a painting! 'Silly kid,' Harry thought but it was nice to get this sort of reaction and Harry was getting a real kick out of showing him things. When Harry pointed out the ladies in their swimwear he thought Tom would flip. He leapt up and down and turned round and round like he was dancing on a sand dollar.

They were so content lazing around and people watching that the boys were unaware of time passing when suddenly Harry thought, Oh Lord the provisions, I almost forgot. Grabbing Tom's hand he said that it was so late they would have to cut across the big garden. Harry helped his brother over the wall and looking around carefully, made sure it was all clear. It was, so the boys took off at a run for the other side of the lawn. They were half way across when they heard the barking and two large dogs appeared from around the side of the house, coming straight for them. Tom froze but Harry took his hand and pulled him along until they reached the trees. Harry shouted to Tom to get up the tree quickly, then launched himself after his little brother and started climbing. Tom was huddled paralysed with fear on a low branch, too scared to move. Harry had to climb over him and then pull him up higher out of danger. Harry tried to calm his frightened sibling as he sat, eyes closed, hands clamped to his ears to keep out the terrible barking. Harry watched the two dogs frantically leaping at the tree, time and time again, cart wheeling backwards and then coming at them once more. Harry held Tom close and said not to worry, that the dogs would go away soon. But they didn't.

They watched the sun set, taking away the warmth as it shot reds, oranges and golds across the sky, the colours filtering through the leaves before finally following the sun.

Harry told Tom the story of the Mighty Orca whose job it was to pull the ball of fire into the sea every evening to douse its glow. After a while Tom started shivering and Harry held him tighter and rubbed his arms and back to warm him.

The dogs had quietened down now and simply sat looking up at the Boscobelle boys. Harry didn't say he was scared but he was. Even if they got away now, his mother would be frantic with worry and livid. At least he wouldn't go home empty handed as the tree held many mangoes, the large perfumed kind that with one bite made you think you were in heaven. Harry had picked a few to take with them and handed one to Tom to eat. Suddenly there was a shrill whistle, the dogs ears pricked up and they were off heading back to the house. Harry grasped Tom's hand and clambering down they set off as fast as their legs could carry them in the opposite direction.

As the weary, cold lads at last neared home Harry heard his pals shouting 'Boscobelle!' and they ran to meet them. White Boy (because he was so light coloured) spoke first saying they were in deep trouble and that their mummy was gonna whip their hides when they got back. When White Boy asked where they had been all that while, Harry quickly told their story with a few embellishments that made Tall Boy (because he was so tall) go "Ooh and Aah" and Teet (because of his stick out teeth) suck on them and chupse with wonder at their adventure.

Their mother was furious when they arrived home, but it didn't last. She was too relieved and thankful to have her boys back again, safe and sound, and she was soon cuddling them both. Then they all sat down to munch on their mangoes and Harry started to retell the adventure but she said he was to finish eating first.

"How many times do I have to tell you Harry hard ears? No well brought up Bajan green monkey ever speaks with his mouth full!"

58

The Wild Life Reserve was cool and shady, a welcoming relief from the blistering sun. I had a cold drink and sat for a while in the shade; there was not a single monkey in sight. Eventually I got up and made my way along a narrow path through the trees and suddenly the air was filled with screeching and chattering. Turning a bend I came across some of the reasons for all the noise. It was obviously feeding time and the animals had all gathered for a fruit and vegetable feast; huge tortoises were climbing over each other to get to the food. Actually, I noticed on closer inspection, that many of these pre-historic giants were ignoring the food and just climbing over each other; they were very noisy lovers. There were two stone benches nearby which would have been nice to sit on but each was already taken, by families of monkeys tucking into their buffet lunch. Wandering back to the path which led towards the bird sanctuary, my progress was slowed considerably by the large shelled creatures in front, wise enough to know the correct walking pace for such a climate. I made several sketches on my pad, especially of the baby monkeys, before I reluctantly left the reserve. It was as I was driving past a gully on the way home in the twilight, that I heard the chattering again and looking up into a tree saw a mother monkey and her two babies eating juicy sweet smelling mangoes.

I was still driving through the country when it got dark, having tried a short cut which as usual in Barbados became a dead end. Having got lost again, I now roughly had my bearings, simply by keeping the red shot sunset seas of the west coast in view. But when it got dark in the country it was like someone pulling a black curtain down. Bragadung! I took a right turn which I thought would lead onto the coast road but instead the lane got narrower; it was pitch black but my lights picked up a bend ahead. As I drove round it, I almost crashed into a man who ran out of the cane field. I slammed on the brakes, sure that I'd hit him and the engine failed. But the man was all right, he'd stopped, his hands braced on the bonnet and stared at me for the longest seconds, eyes hate-filled and menacing. He lifted his hands and slammed them down again on the bonnet making me jump, then just as quickly he was gone into the cane field on the opposite side of the lane. The blackness and sudden silence around me was unnerving. No star lit the sky, no tree frog or cricket sounded. I tried once, twice to start the engine and I don't mind telling you I was getting really nervous; then on the third try it started. I turned the car and took off as fast as I could. Blow the coast road, I would take the highway back to Bridgetown. The hairs on the back of my neck were standing until I reached the highway and I did not take my foot off the accelerator until I got home. Tucked up safely in my flat again, I realised I'd passed only one or two cars all the way back and thought how odd that the roads were so empty. It's a good job that I don't believe in ghosts and ghouls because if I did believe in such nonsense, this would certainly be the night they walked. My sleep that night was fitful. Oddly shaped shadows moved across my room and when I did sleep I had the most terrible nightmare, which I'd forgotten entirely by morning.

It was a long time before I could get that cane field man's face out of my mind. It kept coming back to haunt me. Truly, I had never seen such evil.

GOD DON'T SLEEP

Clyde woke suddenly, knocking over the chair his feet had been resting on and sat straight up, an unreasonable fear gripping him. Someone had been staring at him through the window while he slept; he was sure of it! But now all he could see was the shadow of the tree branches dancing across the window pane in the light of the dying sun. Was it a dream then? Was it fingers of mahogany tapping to come in? Or was it fingers...? He shook his head trying to make sense of his jumbled thoughts but it only made his head ache from the morning rum session worse. He got up and crossed to the sink for some cold water to revive him, kicking the chair aside as he went. The water helped and he became aware of a hunger gnawing at his belly.

"Woman, where de food is?" he growled.

A stooped old lady finished righting the chair and limped over to place a plate on the table.

"What dis is you old bitch, breadfruit! Where de gravy is den?" The woman cowered, feeling the blow before it struck, and as she hit the floor, she curled herself into a ball in a vain attempt to protect her belly, which still screamed at her from the last beating. Shivering, the old lady braced herself for the kick which would follow. His foot caught her spine and she lay very still; not daring to move because the pain was intense and she knew from experience, the slightest movement would be like a red hot poker in her back. She stayed still also because if she did not, then it would draw the man's attention to her again and provoke another attack. This man she called husband would one day kill her, she knew that for certain and she longed for death like the dry earth longs for rain. If any humanity had remained in her she would have ended this hell called life herself but she had become inanimate like the earth, incapable even of making the decision to take her own miserable life.

Clyde ate the food, shaved and splashed Limacol on his cheeks. He looked into the broken mirror and picked his teeth with a hibiscus twig. He seemed pleased with himself. She watched him through half closed eyes, hardly daring to breathe as he put on his suit, clean shirt and the shoes she had polished, willing him away quickly so that she could tend to her wounds. The wooden house was quite bare now, denuded over the years of anything of value for the price of a bottle of rum. Hanging around the wall on a string were some of the man's clothes, kept clean and smart. The woman's wardrobe was what she was wearing, tattered remnants of curtains that once hung at the windows of her pristine home. She hadn't had shoes for years, which was just as well as none could have fitted over her swollen feet. At last her husband was ready to go and opening the door, he left without a backward glance.

Some time later the woman opened her eyes. Incredibly she felt no pain, just a pleasant warmth all over her body. A strange light glowed in the room. "Sunset already?" Then, as if in answer, a beautiful face smiled down at her. She knew she would be all right now.

Clyde moved out of the bush surrounding his house, walking with a spring in his step, past the old well by the broken tree and onto the track that led through the sugar cane. He pulled his shoulders back as he approached the top of Porters Hill and started down the Gap where the fat woman lived. She was bathing at the pipe, as he knew she would be, after a hard day's labour. When she caught sight of him she stood up, pulling the towel round her as he passed. What he wouldn't give to get his hands on those bubbies or rub soap on that big botsie.

"What you staring at you dirty old man? You want I should get me husband to you? G'along wicha!"

He smirked back at her. She hadn't been quick enough with the towel and he'd gloated over her large pendulous breasts before she'd had time to straighten up and cover herself. He walked on down the hill, adjusting his erection, feeling horny and as he passed some shak shak trees was wondering if he should give himself a hand job, when he jumped with fear at a rustling sound close by. His first thought was that the woman's husband had come after him but as he peered back, he saw a little girl walking away looking over her shoulder at him. He thought she looked familiar but the darkness engulfed her before he could remember where he'd seen her before. The man reached the bottom of the hill and waited for traffic to clear before he could cross but as the bus to Sandridge went by full of people, he was surprised to see the familiar face at one of the windows looking straight at him. It was her again, the same girl. A car blasted its horn, nearly running him over as he watched after the disappearing bus. Shaken, he reached the path and walked towards Billy's Bar, passing the big up's homes where the white people lived, with the tall walls surrounding them, so you couldn't see through to the sea any more. One house had large electric gates and a lot of young men were liming in front of them.

The bar was full when Clyde arrived. He ordered a bottle of rum and took it with a glass to a table in the corner, nodding to a couple of men as he went. When the waitress walked by he grasped her arm and offered her a drink which she declined, pulling away in obvious disgust.

"Stuck up bitch," Clyde thought. "What I wouldn't like to do to you one night!" He sat on, drinking and musing about the waitress. Where did she live? How did she get home? Did she walk alone? And feeling the old excitement rise, he decided he would follow her that night when the bar closed. Clyde thought about how he would give it to her, hoping she would fight. He liked that. He felt for the thick twine he always carried in his pocket. He would come out of the cane softly, the twine would be round her neck before she heard a thing. She would pass out and he would drag her deeper into the cane. Tonight, he felt lucky.

"What was that?" A movement outside the window had caught his eye. Nothing. Nobody there. "What de hell is wrong wid you tonight?" he scolded himself. He was nervous as a virgin. He smiled. He liked virgins. Lifting the glass, his peripheral vision caught movement. "Who was that?" The rum spilt over his hand as he brought the glass down with a thump. Who was just looking at him through the doorway? It was that damned girl again! Clyde leapt up and ran to the door, looking out right and left but she'd gone. He returned to the table, slumped back into the chair and poured more rum. The people at the bar were watching him, like he was a mad man, like he was dirt! He glared back at them and they averted their eyes. "Ha! Wimps. Girly boys, the lot of 'em'. He drained his glass. "Who the devil was that girl?"

Most of the people had left Billy's Bar as Clyde sat getting more drunk. It was a quiet place now. A few regulars called in but left quite quickly. There was an uneasiness in the air that night, like a hurricane was brewing. Some people said so. It was certainly hot enough. Maybe they felt a chill as the eyes of the old man slid over them but nobody seemed in a congenial mood. Something made them want to get off home to the family. Clyde was sleeping with his head on his arms when the waitress shook him and said he must leave as they were closing. He looked longingly at the bottle but it was empty; he was sure he'd left some. The bitch had probably taken it. He staggered outside into a humidity that put a strangle hold on breathing.

Waiting in the bushes across the road for the waitress and Billy to lock up and leave, Clyde was urinating onto the leaves when he heard voices. Billy and the waitress were standing talking. Then Billy called out something to her, turned and walked away towards Speightstown. Good, she was alone! He would follow her home. Clyde could feel the excitement growing in his loins as he watched

her and began to plan his moves, twisting the twine in his pocket. Then a car drew up alongside her and she got in, leaning over to kiss the driver before they drove away.

Bitch! Bitch! Bitch! The fury built inside Clyde threatening to choke him. But wait, there was the little girl again. This time she was beckoning him back along the road, smiling. Where had he seen her before? He felt he knew her, but just couldn't quite place it. 'Who cares anyway? Such a little thing, just how I like 'em.' A wheezing chuckle spilled out and was whisked away by an impulsive breeze which took his words along too. 'If they're big enough, they're old enough!' He picked up the pace and went after her. Back up the Gap she went and he followed, climbing the hill; the girl always a spit ahead, turning and smiling always beckoning him onwards. He was getting out of breath, whether it was with excitement or too much rum he didn't know but he knew he mustn't let this little girl out of his sight. She was so young. How old? Eleven, twelve maybe, sweet, ripe for the plucking. So much better than the old bitch at the bar.

Along the cane track now, the moonlight cast eerie shadows onto the rough earth through the cane blades. She had started running and he could hear her giggling as she turned and urged him onwards. 'Prick teaser! Just you wait little girl!' Clyde burst out of the cane field and nearly got run over by a car. His hands were on the bonnet, a red rage came over him as he stared in at the frightened face of the driver. A primal urge to kill the man surged through him but then he saw her again in the field on the other side of the lane. So he slammed his hands onto the bonnet and raced after her. Shortly he had to stop, bent over, his breath coming in painful bursts. When finally he could look up again and take stock of his whereabouts, she was gone. He clenched his fists in his rage and frustration and he pummelled them into the ground, finally slumping down with his back against the wall of the old well.

When he opened his eyes she was back again. Her sweet face was smiling. Except that as he watched the smile change, her face was altering and becoming more familiar. It all came back to him now like a bolt out of the blue and he stood up in terror. He was taken back all those years to the night he forced this little girl to the same place at knife point. It was right here that he had beaten, raped and strangled her. Afterwards it had been so easy to drop the child's body down the well. Then he threw boulders on top to cover his crime. It never even occurred to him that he would get caught. After all it wasn't the first time he'd murdered, far from it. And it was always so easy.

When, after several weeks, someone eventually found the child and the authorities brought her up, a large crowd had gathered. Clyde was one of them. He had looked into the battered face that water and time had made grotesque and cried real tears with the rest of the onlookers. He looked now into that same face as her grin widened into a rictus and she advanced towards him. Clyde became aware that they were not alone. There was movement all around, behind the tree, blocking the moon, a hundred faces, children, girls, boys, women, all crowding in, all advancing towards him. He recognised some of them; objects of his sexual arousal, victims of his need to inflict the utmost pain and terror in order to assuage that lust. Among the advancing procession was the bent form of his wife and for a brief second Clyde thought he was saved, but then as she got closer he noticed that like all the others, she had no substance.

"What goes around, comes around husband." She hissed close to his ear, "But all's well that ends well."
She chuckled and the others pressed closer too; his pants filled and hot urine coursed down his legs. They were right on him now, mouths gaping, steamy foul air escaped and curled its tendrils around him. He stared into the dark cavernous hell holes and felt the demons reaching for him, pulling him inside. Clyde couldn't breathe; his chest was tight; they were suffocating him. The faces opened and drew him into a terrible blackness and finally, losing his balance, he was pitched backwards into the murky abyss of the

well. His scream went with him all the way down and it seemed a very long way. The pain as he slammed onto the bottom was so excruciating he couldn't move. Something was sticking into the side of his head and he realised it was the bone from his own arm which had been torn completely off. His wife's face appeared to him again, looking young and lovely as she had when they first met. "God don't sleep Clyde."

His cries grew fainter through the night. The only person close enough to hear would have been his own wife in the nearby house but Daddy Death had called earlier to take her home. Only her broken, lifeless body remained on the floor where Clyde had left her earlier that evening.

The night was very still, not a leaf stirred. Tree frogs were silent as though waiting for something; crickets rubbed their legs silently in anticipation and the stars were hard bright eyes that dared people to venture from their homes. A few rough boys heard strange sounds and wanted to go out, but old grannies who knew things forbade it. They said that it was the night when the spirits roamed and small boys could disappear like puffs of smoke.

Granny spoke to granny in soft whispers of Baccou, Steel Donkey, Rollin' Calf, Mama Malade and others. But they all agreed that whatever roamed that night would put even these to flight.

Clyde was quite dead when a barking dog brought his owner to the well the following day and word soon spread. The people gathered quickly and there were many, for this was Barbados. They all agreed that the look on Clyde's face was one of pure terror; eyes wide and mouth fixed in a silent scream. They said every single bone in his body must be broken and when the police brought him up, one arm was still missing. Nobody would go down the well again to retrieve it. Granny nodded knowingly to granny and they said to each other,

'God don't sleep!'

My unreasonable terrors of the previous night and a restless sleep haunted by visions of the canefield man's face, were nothing but bad dreams and in the bright morning sunshine all seemed right with the world again.

It was Saturday and I was in a quandary. My friends had invited me to the races at The Garrison, but England was playing a one day cricket match against the West Indies at Kensington Oval, and that was where I really wanted to be. Eventually I decided to do both. I would spend the morning watching cricket, get a taxi to the Garrison for a couple of races and then back for the last few overs. That way I wouldn't feel that I'd let any friends down. I was like an excited schoolboy driving to Kensington Oval and couldn't help thinking how Dad would have felt the same. A dour man by nature, cricket was the only thing I had ever seen him get remotely excited about. I had grown up loving the game with a passion and besides England, the team I had always supported was The West Indies. As a boy I'd sat glued to the television as Curtley Ambrose and Courtney Walsh had bowled their finest; they were the greatest ever in my opinion, with Brian Lara the best batsman, although Dad said Sir Donald Bradman had been the one who had earned that accolade. I had just loved the wicked glares Curtley gave the batsmen and watched with fascination as a kaleidoscope of expressions contorted Courtney's face. All gone now sadly and the current team's performance left a lot to be desired but their day would come again. England, on the other hand was doing well for a change so it should be a good match.

The police directed me to park in Mannings yard, just opposite the entrance and as I had already purchased my ticket for the Sir Garfield Sobers stand, I could meander through the crowds, soaking up the atmosphere. The locals were laughing, joking, eating and calling out to the English who were answering with equal fervour. As I passed the stalls selling cricket paraphernalia, food and drink, the aromas made my stomach rumble. I bought a local newspaper whose headlines blared that a man's body had been found down a well but I wanted the sports pages at the back. I climbed some stairs and was soon gazing down on the pitch. The ground was so much smaller than I had envisaged but I liked that, I felt close to the action and it felt friendly. I stopped by a bar and bought two beers and some flying fish cutters liberally coated with hot sauce which I took down to my seat, right at the front. I was in seventh heaven. I was actually here, sitting at the famous Kensington Oval, the beer was good and cold, and the sandwiches delicious. What more could a man want? As I munched away I looked at the crowds pouring in and everyone who sat nearby greeted me warmly. Was it because I had no family now that I felt the warmth of these people so deeply? Whatever it was I had never felt alone here since I arrived. In fact, I actually felt that I belonged especially with Cecily and her family; they made me feel like one of their own and I spent a lot of time with them.

Half-way through the morning, the game was in full swing and the teams were taking a drinks break. I took out my binoculars and trained them on the Kensington stand where there was a lot of noise going on. A musical group had arrived and everyone seemed to be in party mood. My neighbour explained that it was Mac Fingal's band. I scanned the people. It was fascinating; they were drinking, laughing, singing. One man was blowing into a conch shell and another with one arm danced round to a radio carried under his stump. My neighbour, who was a mine of information, told me the man was called "Oney" which needed no explanation. Some women wearing the shortest shorts I had ever seen were gyrating sensually, drinking beer and, as the Bajans would say, "acting foolish". Everyone was having so much fun. All at once I caught a familiar face in the crowd. It was my friend the old man with the swanky outfits. He was smoking his pipe and wearing a bright yellow suit that day. I waved to him, realising that he would never be able to see me but I did it anyway. To my astonishment the old fellow waved back at me with a little Union Jack flag in his hand.

Returning my attention to the game, my neighbour spoke to me again, pointing at my red burning knees. It was so breezy that I hadn't felt the heat of the sun's rays, even though our half of the stand was now bathed in brilliant sunshine. Luckily I had some long trousers in my bag for the races and decided to change into them immediately.

It was so hard to drag myself away from the cricket but a promise is a promise and I wouldn't let my pals down. The taxi, having picked its way slowly through the crowds, had at long last arrived at the Garrison. My friend Richard had said to meet him upstairs in his father's box. I pushed my way through an excited, voluble and good natured crowd, up the steps, through the members' bar and the restaurant to the boxes. Richard's Dad's box was air conditioned which was wonderful after the heat outside. It had its own bar, plenty of food on offer and a large outside terrace overlooking the track. Richard had some other pals with him from England, and they were already well into the champagne, so I quickly joined them and made up for lost time. I was glad though when after a while Richard suggested we go to the members' bar which was much more atmospheric, bustling and friendly. I stood at the large windows and watched a couple of races. Then I spotted the hat and yellow suit below me, sitting in the crowd. The old gentleman, like me, must have decided not to miss either sporting event. This time I was determined to speak to him. I pushed my way through the door and down the steps but when I got to the spot the yellow suit had gone. Disappointed, I asked one of the punters where the man had gone. "What man?" he asked. I described the old fellow in detail and got annoyed when the punter and his friends fell about laughing. I couldn't understand what was so funny and thought their behaviour quite rude. My annoyance must have shown in my face because the man spoke again. "You telling

King Dyal

D. Stuart

us you just saw de King? Man you must think we're rass'ole idiots!" I left them still laughing and went back to my pals in the bar. We had several rums, and then more champagne, back in the box, by which time I realised it was too late to get back to the cricket and that I was no longer in any fit state to move far. I told Richard about the old man and the reaction I'd got from the crowd below and Richard repeated the story to his father. I could have sworn he too quickly killed a smile; didn't actually laugh though.

Then he explained. "Duncan, no wonder they all laughed. They probably thought you were trying to make fun of them. You see the man you describe is Redvers Dundonald Dyall, more commonly known as King Dyall. He was one of the most famous characters around for years.

Dressed just as you've said, rode his old bike everywhere. He sat exactly where you said you saw him today and was always in the Kensington stand at cricket. Used to incense the Barbadians around him because he always supported the English team."

"Why are you talking about him in the past tense?" I asked.

He studied my obviously concerned face and said quietly, "Trouble is old man, he's been dead for years!"

It's a funny thing though and I've thought about this a lot. As Richard's father spoke to me I almost knew what was coming. I tried to sort out the thoughts in my booze-fuddled brain but nothing made sense.

I simply mumbled, "Must have read about him I suppose." Although I knew I hadn't. I didn't want him to think I was totally insane, especially as I wasn't too sure myself. I smiled weakly, "Never could take champagne," which was true. They offered to give me a lift home. It was dark as we left the Garrison and some "ladies of the night" as Richard called them, were "strutting their stuff".

Richard rolled down the windows and made lewd suggestions which made the women laugh and make lewder ones back. I hardly noticed; I felt strange.

'TILL DEATH US DO PART

ONE

Waveny tucked into the breakfast of fish cakes and bakes her grandmother had prepared for her. She was a big girl for her age and she loved her food. They lived in a pretty pink wooden house with hooded shutters where fluffy white curtains strewn with pink flowers billowed in the trade winds that kept the place cool. There was one bedroom where Waveny and her grandmother slept and one room which served as kitchen, dining room and lounge. The beautiful mahogany furniture had been made by Waveny's father before he died. A soft comfy settee rested against one wall and was adorned with starched white anti-macassars. Beside this was a small carved table which carried a vase filled with colourful plastic flowers which Waveny had bought Gran for Christmas from Woolworths. Next to this was a small television. Their home was neat and scrupulously clean. The toilet was at the end of the small garden and a vegetable patch bloomed just outside the back door. At the front was a porch with a wooden rocking chair and a small table where Waveny's grandmother sat each day with her morning tea and waved her grand child off to school. She was always there to greet Waveny when she got back and when she was very small Waveny used to think her grand-mother hadn't moved all day. Now she was older; in fact, today was her fourteenth birthday; she realised a lot of work was done while she studied.

Her gran had a morning cleaning job and together with the money Waveny's mother sent from New York every month, it meant they did all right. Waveny looked again at the bright pencil case and coloured pencils that had been her birthday present and grinned.

She thanked her gran again, kissed her cheek and picking up her school bag set off down the Gap to catch the bus.

Walking down the hill she passed the house in the trees where the white couple lived. They were a bit of a puzzle, keeping themselves to themselves, rarely going out except for their daily sea bath. This information was according to gran and was via the couple's maid. They were English and writers of some kind but nearly every time Waveny passed, the woman was outside on the deck with her easel painting, always wearing a different bikini. She had long blonde hair tied high on top of her head and when Waveny waved, the woman always waved back. Gran said it was disgusting, a woman her age dressed like that; she had two grown daughters after all. But Waveny thought it was cool. The couple were still like young lovers too after all those years together and that was what Waveny wanted more than anything in the whole world. To fall in love and marry 'till death do us part'. She liked that bit. She wanted a good man who she could set up a nice home with and rear children who would be loved, happy and most important, would always have their mummy and daddy around.

Still daydreaming, she neared the bus stop and her thoughts naturally progressed to HIM. Every day as she stood waiting she wondered about him and thought such silly things: is he going to be there? Will there be a seat nearby so that I can study him undetected? Which tie will he be wearing? She felt her heart quicken as the bus from St. Albans came into view and by the time it stopped, her face felt hot and trickles of sweat dribbled into the shirt collar of her school uniform. Waiting her turn to get on board, she dabbed at her temples with a cloth she always carried and kept her eyes on the floor, as she walked past the seats, swivelling sidelong glances until she caught sight of his brown shoes and black briefcase. Incredibly the seat next to him was vacant. Her instinctive reaction was to move on but summoning all her courage she sat down next to him, her eyes firmly fixed on the cloth which she was twisting nervously between her fingers. Waveny could hardly breathe as they were carried on their way.

The bus lurched and came to a standstill at the next stop and out of nowhere there was a white paper bag under her nose.

"Would you like a sweet?"
The deep melodious voice touched something way down deep inside her that she didn't understand but found very exciting.
"No thank you," she replied, eyes still on her lap. But how could she eat when her heart was already in her mouth?

He told her that his name was Mark, that he had noticed her several times before and asked what school she went to and what she wanted to do when she left! With so many questions being fired at her, she had to lift her eyes to his or he would think her very rude. He told her how important school was if she wanted a good life. Mark said he had an important job in Bridgetown with a big accountancy firm and being only nineteen, he was very young for such a high position. Mark, (she kept repeating the name over and over in her mind as his melodious voice continued), had started work two months previously which was about the time she had first noticed him. Waveny hardly heard a word he said although she tried to keep focused and nod in the right places. She just kept losing herself in his dark liquid eyes, marvelling at the incredibly long curly lashes, his tiny ears like shells and such white even teeth. She watched his pink tongue darting, wondered how those full sensuous lips would feel on her own and flushed hotly thinking he must have read her thoughts.

All too soon the bus reached her stop and she felt so despondent but as she got up to leave Mark said, "See you tomorrow Waveny, I'll keep your seat." Her feet hardly seemed to touch the ground on her way to school and all day she was in such a state of intense excitement that she couldn't concentrate on anything. First love, with all its passion, excitement and pain, had pierced her young vulnerable heart.

They met daily from then on and talked of many things. Gran often commented on her high spirits and put it down to a school girl crush on a teacher, especially as Waveny was getting all her homework done and going to bed early without going out to play.

Waveny wished the time away until she stood, watching with excitement as the St. Abans bus approached each day. Then one fine morning Mark said that he would be having the entire day off that coming Thursday and he invited her to join him at the beach, saying that afterwards he would buy them a meal at Chefette, in Holetown. He said that they could sit at a table right next to the beach and watch the sunset. The idea was outrageous. Go to the beach with a man? For a whole day? Have a meal at The Chefette? She had seen the rich people eating there but had never thought she could be one of them. If only she dare. To be with her prince, wasn't that worth everything? Waveny decided she was prepared to move heaven and earth to spend the entire day with Mark.

It was the very first time she had ever lied to her gran when she said she was going to her friend's house after school to study and would have tea with her afterwards. She wrote a letter to the headmistress explaining her absence was due to illness then signing gran's name to it, gave the note to her friend to hand to the teacher. Never had she felt such excitement.

Her day with Mark was the happiest of her life. They swam, well he swam and tried to teach her how to improve her dog paddle. After a while he made her put on his mask and introduced her to another world, one of coral reefs and multi-coloured fish that darted about in the mosaic patterns of the sun that filtered through the blue water. He showed her French Angelfish that he said only spoke in patois; Damsel Fish swimming with dozens of Blue Chromis, a Trumpet Fish he called Satchmo and Queen Parrot Fish that ruled over their realm by squawking like birds, or so he said. Mark pointed out Surgeon Fish and Doctor Fish, telling her never to get ill on a Thursday as this was their day off from the Queen Elizabeth Hospital. Her jaws ached with laughing. Future times, he promised, he would find the Balloon Fish, Goat Fish or Flying Gurnard for her and if they were very lucky and she got good enough to swim to the coral gardens further out, they might meet the tiny Highhat or Fred Astaire as Mark called it. 'Future times' was the phrase that lodged in Waveny's heart.

She was filled with awe and energy as they walked along the beach and found shelter from the hot noonday sun under some casuarina trees. They lay on their backs looking up through the feathery branches at the new leaves, so green and brilliant they hurt the eyes. Mark had brought some cokes and coconut bread; Waveny couldn't believe how hungry she was and what a wonderful feeling of well-being had come over her. He leaned up on his elbow and looked at her with those dark eyes and then he brought his lips to hers and his tongue started to explore her mouth. She literally jumped as Mark's hands went to her breasts and then quickly down to her mound which he squeezed gently and she thought she would explode. Waveny felt what seemed like a current race through her body, from her tingling lips through her hard nipples right down to where she felt a dampness between her legs that she knew wasn't sea water. The thrill was so great that she knew she could refuse this man nothing. He was trying to free her breasts from the swimsuit when some tourists walked by, peering in at them, so Mark stopped and sat up.

Waveny said that the interruption was just as well, explaining that she wanted to save herself for her husband and certainly did not want to get pregnant. This seemed to make Mark angry and he wouldn't speak for some time which made Waveny sad and unsure of herself. Eventually he turned to her, held her close and whispered words of love. He said of course they would marry, but he explained that he could get into serious trouble at the moment as Waveny was under age. He suggested that perhaps they shouldn't see each other for a while. At this Waveny became distraught and started to cry. He dried her tears, thought for a while and then said that if she did get pregnant, their respective families would have to accept that they were in love and would have to let them get married immediately. "Til death us do part," he added, smiling and kissing her salty lips. He pulled her to her feet for another swim.

Later, after chicken and fries at Chefette, they sipped their cokes and watched the huge red sun fall into the water and splash its colours over the surface. She felt so grown up and couldn't help hoping that one of her school friends would pass by and see her in such a grand restaurant. They spoke of love, of eternity and of children. There and then they decided on a white wedding and swore their devotion, "Till death us do part." Their love was absolute and Waveny was the happiest girl in the world. When they strolled back in the moonlight to their place on the beach, this time there was no holding back. He touched every nerve in her body, his fingers and tongue brought sensations that made her wild with desire and when he entered her, although it hurt a bit at first she was soon lost in an explosion of sensations. She really did think she had died and gone to heaven.

It was after they met secretly several more times that Waveny missed her period, and when she told Mark that morning on the bus he was just as happy as she was. She wanted to tell her Gran and his parents straight away but Mark explained that he had to go away to his company's head office overseas for a couple of weeks. He said while he was away she could start making plans for the wedding. Then when Mark returned they would gather his parents and her gran together to tell them the good news. He gave her his mother's address and telephone number in Six Men's Village and said he would write as soon as he arrived.

Of course he never did write. A very confused old man lived at the address in Six Men's Village. The telephone number turned out to be a bar in St. Peter, and Waveny visited several accountancy firms in Bridgetown, all that she could find in the telephone book, but none had a Mark working for them or anyone who met with the description she gave.

Finally came the awful realisation that she had to tell Gran, the woman who had given her so much, that she had let her down badly. Her gran was broken hearted; she had wanted so much more for her grand daughter. Waveny left school and soon afterwards the baby was born. Then Gran's diabetes worsened and she became very ill, eventually having to have a leg amputated. After Gran came out of the hospital, work was out of the question so Waveny took over her cleaning job while her gran took care of the baby.

Things were very tough. The lovely little house soon began to look bedraggled, her baby needed new clothes and often, Waveny couldn't afford her grandmother's medication. Still through it all there was magic in Waveny's life, from the day her baby was born and placed into her arms she marvelled at the tiny thing that was her total responsibility, whose life was literally in her hands. The love she felt immediately for her child overwhelmed her, was all encompassing and gripped her heart with a special hold that would never loosen for as long as she drew breath. She named her daughter Madonna, after the pop star.

When Madonna was two they got a letter from Waveny's mother in New York to say that she was remarrying and that, as she now had a new family to take care of, she would be unable to send any more money home. Waveny looked at her gran, who seemed to have aged twenty years in the last two and then she looked at Madonna who smiled up with her dark liquid eyes and long curly lashes. She bent to kiss her tiny shell like ears and hearing her baby's tummy grumbling, the way ahead became clear. She was no longer prepared to go on this way, no more hunger, no more rags for her baby. From now on, only the very best would be good enough for her child. Madonna would go to the best schools, be dressed in the finest clothes. She would succeed in life and never would she be caught by some man as Waveny had been. Whatever was needed to be done Waveny would do, to ensure her child's happiness and success in life. It was at that moment the decision was made to enlist in the world's oldest profession, to join the girls who frequented the Garrison and Nelson Street area. Never again would she or hers want for anything.

Although her grandmother must have guessed almost right away where all the extra money was suddenly coming from she never spoke about it and when Madonna was old enough to ask, Waveny told her that she worked in a fashion house and spent the evenings modelling or helping out in a friend's bar. Waveny was very good at what she did and soon she was renting her own apartment near the Garrison to accommodate a large regular clientele. She was bright, amusing and very inventive. As hundreds of men thumped themselves into her and she giggled and screamed when appropriate, smiled and told them how good they were, how big they were, her hatred for the male sex grew with every thrust.

TWO

Very soon the family wanted for nothing financially, Madonna's education taking priority. The pretty child had grown into a beautiful teenager who turned heads wherever she went but despite this she was not vain or self absorbed. She was a good girl and when her mother sat her down to lecture about the evils that men do, which happened fairly often, she listened patiently, then politely told her mother that she had no time for boys, only for study. At eighteen, all her hard work paid off when she was rewarded with a scholarship to study law overseas.

Madonna became a top student who regularly wrote long, gossipy letters home about college, friends and the wonders of America. Then one day three life altering events happened to

Waveny. Her grandmother, who had been hospitalised for weeks, finally succumbed to the infections that had taken over her body and died; Waveny found out that she was HIV positive and Madonna wrote to say she was quitting college to come home and get married. It was the last piece of news that upset Waveny most.

Three weeks later saw Waveny rocking herself in her grandmother's chair on the porch just as her gran had always done. She sipped from a glass of wine, deep in thought. The bottle stood on the table with another glass awaiting Madonna's arrival. After a while she heard the taxi coming up the Gap and stood up. As Madonna got out of the car, her mother's heart leapt at the beautiful woman standing before her; then she rushed to hug her daughter. Lord but she had missed her so much. With the taxi paid and away, the two women sipped their wine, touching all the while as though making sure the other was still there. They gossiped about everything carefully avoiding the subject that was uppermost in their minds.

Madonna had tried hard to hide her initial shock at her mother's appearance. Waveny had got thin and looked more like sixty-six than thirty six. She remembered all the sacrifices her mother had made for her; the long hours at the fashion house. She knew her mother must be bitterly disappointed and Madonna burned with guilt. But when the love of your life comes along, what can a person do? She would look after Waveny now and pay back in some small measure all her mother had done for her. She knew she would have a battle on her hands regarding the marriage, but she would go gently and try to make Waveny understand what it meant to be in love.

She began by telling her mother that she was still a virgin and was saving herself for her wedding night, something she knew Waveny most wanted to hear.

"Mummy, Philip has old fashioned values, like you and wants a pure woman for his wife." She explained that she had met her fiancee when she'd been sent to a law firm for work experience;

he and several partners owned the company and although he was a much older man he was kind and gentle. She clasped her hands and her eyes got a far away look.

"He is also good looking, sophisticated and everything I ever wanted in a husband. Mummy, that first date – you should have seen the flowers he sent; the beautiful restaurant he took me to for dinner. And all the waiters knew him!"

Madonna poured her heart out to Waveny and said she just couldn't resist him or his romantic marriage proposal. It was almost too good to be true when he told her he wanted to move his operations lock, stock and barrel to an off-shore company in Barbados so that they could look after Waveny's mother. Also, he'd added, almost as an afterthought, he could save on taxes.

He promised that if Madonna wanted, she could finish her studies at a later date but right now he needed her to return home to plan their large wedding and buy the biggest fanciest house on the Royal Westmoreland Golf Course. He wanted to be able to play first thing in the mornings. He was having his Rolls Royce sent over but wanted her to choose whatever colour she liked from the latest Mercedes range which Simpsons, the local dealer, would import for her.

Madonna stopped talking at last and laughed at her mother's gaping mouth.

"Oh yes, I forgot to tell you Mummy," really enjoying her mother's expression, "he's also extremely wealthy."

Waveny was truly astonished when her daughter told her that the home and car would be in her name (for tax reasons) and that a small fortune had been deposited in her bank account, enough to pay for the biggest wedding Barbados had ever seen, with a sufficient amount left to last two lifetimes. How could Waveny not be glad for her daughter? It seemed that she had found a decent man, a species that Waveny hadn't believed existed. A saint! She smiled to herself. And it helped that he was sitting on a pot of gold! Her baby would never want for anything.

THREE

Philip Manley, Waveny's future son-in-law arrived four months later, by which time Waveny and Madonna had moved into the immaculately furnished house at Westmoreland. Philip checked into the Sandy Lane Hotel until after the wedding, as he insisted he wanted everything to be proper and above board, and in any event, he had many business transactions to complete before the happy day.

Although retired now, Waveny thought she should go and say a last good bye to her old friends at the Garrison. She especially wanted to see the teenager she had befriended a couple of years earlier, mainly because she had reminded Waveny of herself. She would also be able to give the girl some money to help out. Mary was very pleased to see Waveny and immediately made some tea and brought out the sweet cakes so that they could curl up on her settee and catch up with the gossip, just like old times.

Waveny finally broke the news to Mary that she was leaving for another island. Mary was so upset that she cried for a long time while Waveny held her and comforted her. When the tears were dry, Waveny cheered the girl up by telling her that she had paid the rent on the apartment to the end of the month and that Mary could use it until then. Waveny felt bad about lying to Mary about leaving the island but she had to cut all ties with her former profession. Nothing from her past must be allowed to pop up in the future and spoil her daughter's happiness. But Mary was the only memory from that past that she would cherish and worry about from time to time. Before Waveny left, Mary put her fingers to her lips and grinning with childlike delight, pulled her over to the crack in the door.

Stifling giggles, she showed Waveny her new client who the

other girls were busy preparing for her. Mary whispered, "He's a bit kinky but pays really well." Waveny looked through at the trick. He was naked, his hands and feet were tied to the bed posts and he was looking longingly at the wall where Mary's paraphernalia of a dominatrix hung waiting. The women smiled and hugged each other and Waveny promised to forward her new address, a promise that would never materialise. She walked away without a backward glance. She was leaving this old life behind for good. Her new life, what was left of it, lay ahead and she was going to enjoy herself.

Philip was invited to dinner by Madonna to see his new house a week later, so that he could meet his future mother-in-law at last. Madonna introduced the two most important people in her life to each other and sheer happiness glowed from Waveny's precious daughter's beautiful face. The meal was perfect and afterwards Madonna gave her fiancee a tour of the home that he had lavished money on without ever having seen. He was delighted with everything and assured his future mother-in-law that he would make Madonna the happiest girl in the world. Waveny eventually excused herself and went to bed early saying how tired she felt with all the excitement.

The wedding was the most lavish celebration ever seen on the island. All the big ups were there, politicians, ambassadors and rich foreigners. They all stood in stunned silence at St James' Parish Church when Madonna appeared; you could have heard a pin drop; she was so breathtakingly beautiful. Everyone said what a fairy tale couple they made. The bride was like a princess in her long silk gown with its twenty foot train delicately carried by six bridesmaids dressed in colours of the rainbow. The groom, in his white silk suit with tails and top hat, took every woman's eye; he was so handsome. Hundreds of people had gathered outside the church to watch the photographs being taken. As Waveny was standing to one side while the bride and groom posed together, a young white man came towards her, looking puzzled, as though he knew her. Waveny's heart lurched; could he have been one of her customers? Then the man smiled at her and took her picture. The crowd slowly swallowed him but he kept smiling until he vanished in the throng. 'Strange boy' Waveny thought, 'why bother with taking a picture of me when my lovely daughter is standing there?' She soon forgot the incident.

What a party they had afterwards. Philip had taken over Sunbury Plantation House which had been decorated throughout with fresh hibiscus of every colour; tiny lights twinkled in the trees while huge torches spat flames skywards. Krug flowed all night served by a dozen waiters whose job it was to keep the glasses brimming. Entertainment was non stop and featured all the top Caribbean talents together with a couple of American stars. Fresh lobster, salmon and strawberries had been flown in together with huge tins of Beluga caviar which, when added to the local fare, proved a gourmet's delight. For Waveny though, the highlight of the whole day had been when the couple had stood in front of the altar and she heard the words, 'till death us do part'. She sighed contentedly. Her daughter was now married and financially set for life.

At midnight a massive fireworks' display brought the evening to a technicolour climax after which the bands were in full swing and the dancing wild. Nobody could ever remember a better wedding on the island. As the new bride chatted to the guests, Philip whispered in her ear that something had cropped up, and he had to nip back to the office to take an important call from New York. He said to carry on dancing and enjoying herself and that he would see her back at the house later. When he saw the anxious expression on his young bride's face, he kissed her tenderly and told her not to worry, that he would probably arrive home before she did.

Everybody was having such a great time that it was quite late before the bride and her mother could get away but eventually the chauffeur drove them off with much shouting and waving from the remaining guests. What a day it had been and it was great that nobody wanted to leave such a good party.

Philip, in fact, was not home when Madonna and Waveny arrived but they made coffee, got into something comfortable and gossiped about the great event while they waited for the new husband to arrive. Madonna said that she realised this would be the pattern of life living with such a high profile businessman.

The women, like the best friends they were, sat and chatted, watched T.V. and dozed. The coffee perked resolutely through the night as they waited for Philip but when dawn broke and still he had not returned, they telephoned everyone they could think of but nobody knew where he could be. Eventually they informed the police who arrived at the house within fifteen minutes. It was while the officers were taking down details that they got a call from headquarters to say a man's body had been discovered. With dread in their hearts, mother and daughter went with the police to view the corpse which had been found floating in the Careenage. It was Philip. The police said he'd probably been robbed, knifed and pushed into the water. It wasn't the first time something like that had happened. Madonna, naturally was distraught and kept asking what he was doing near The Careenage anyway? The police said his car could have been hijacked on his way to the office. Everybody was stunned at such a tragic ending to a perfect wedding day.

The funeral was a small private affair held at Westbury Cemetery. Madonna was wan and ill looking but Waveny was comforted by the fact that her daughter was young and given time, would get over the death of her husband.

Waveny was the last to walk slowly towards the open coffin. She looked down at the face of her son-in-law. He still looked good even in death. Although she couldn't see his dark liquid eyes any more, his long lashes lay curled on his cheeks and his tiny shell like ears were the image of Madonna's, his daughter. A tear fell onto his lifeless cheek which she brushed away, just as he had swept away the tears of that innocent fourteen year old girl all those years ago.

Waveny had first seen Philip again (or Mark as he would always be to her) through the crack of Mary's door; he was her new client. Of course she hadn't realised then that he was her future son-in-law but she did recognise him as the man who had ruined her life. Later on, at the first dinner in the Westmoreland House, when she was introduced to him, she had nearly died of shock. He hadn't remembered Waveny, naturally. After all, what was there left of that naive fourteen year old who had been so very much in love. Waveny had started to plan her strategy for the wedding day after she excused herself and went to bed that night.

While the fireworks were sending the sky crazy, she had arranged for a threatening letter to be delivered to Philip, supposedly from Mary. Waveny knew he wouldn't be able to refuse the instructions it contained. He couldn't risk losing his respectable business reputation and high social standing for the sake of a little tart. He had made his excuses to Madonna and left for the rendezvous near the Dry Dock at the Careenage. At first he didn't see Waveny in the shadows. When she whispered, 'Hello Mark,' he gazed bewildered into the darkness. Bewilderment rapidly turned to shock as Waveny emerged slowly and recognition finally dawned. In the half light, the face still held elements of the fourteen year old he had met on the bus, seduced and forgotten. He was still staring at her when the blade entered his heart. Afterwards, Waveny had carefully removed Mary's note from his pocket together with the cash before rolling him into the water. She then drove quickly back to the party where nobody had even missed her.

Waveny trailed her fingers along the brass plate engraved with her late son-in-law's name, Philip Mark Manley and whispered, 'Till death us do part. Amen'.

Today I saw the most beautiful wedding in progress as I drove past St. James' church and just had to stop and park. Having pushed my way through the people, I saw the bride who was exquisite, with her bridesmaids posing around her clothed in all the colours of the rainbow and I quickly managed to get off several good shots. The groom was a bit fancy for my taste and I managed nicely to block him out. Then I caught sight of the bride's mother; I knew her from somewhere. When she stood aside I went up to speak to her, ask where we had met but the closer I got the more agitated she became. It was obvious that she didn't know me and looked ready to scream at this stranger homing in on her, so I quickly smiled my most beguiling but before I could turn away, something flashed in my head. At first I thought it must be the photographer's flash lights but it wasn't. It was dark, as though I had my eyes closed and a perfect picture had formed in my mind of my little pink chattel house, curtains blowing. I heard the

The deserted house
& rocking chair

squeaking of the rocker and looked towards it where the bride's mother was sitting, head back, eyes closed. She had a smile on her face as though she was having a nice dream. Wham! The mental picture went and the wedding with all its noises was around me once more. I was still looking into the face of the bride's mother, who by now was looking terrified. I smiled again, reassuringly I hoped, took her photograph and stepped back into the crowd. Now I knew who had lived in my little pink house.

I headed eagerly back to the south coast and Cecily's; I was expected for dinner and I was never late for that. I thought of sharing the vision I'd had at the church with her but she was funny about things like that, superstitious and very religious and the last thing I wanted was to upset Cecily, my surrogate Mum. The thought of her cooking was making my mouth water already and her boys and I needed a good food base because we were going out clubbing afterwards. It was another fabulous evening.

The next morning, my thoughts in gluey shoes, trod a mind maze of dense fog as I tried to get my bearings, still trying to separate dreams from reality but the nightmare had been so real. I was hot, my head throbbed and my mouth was so dry I couldn't move my tongue around. I tried to turn away from the light and promptly fell out of the hammock where I'd obviously spent the night. A feral cat sleeping underneath screeched as she was nearly flattened and exited fast, still spitting at me. I found my keys and opening the door, headed straight for the kitchen. I poured iced water into a jug which I placed on a tray with a glass and added a packet of Paracetamol and some stale coconut cake I had found in the fridge. I went back out onto the patio and sat in the shade on a lounger. Very slowly, my guts stopped churning and my headache subsided a little. How many times since I'd been here had I sworn 'Never again?' I must have consumed more alcohol in the last months than at any time in my entire life before. The only days I stayed reasonably sober were excursion days.

I thought about the King Dyall enigma and wondered if I would see him again. Could the drink be making me hallucinate? I'd heard of pink elephants but old men in coloured suits? And famous old men at that. 'Duncan, my boy, it's a cold shower for you and a shave'. Then perhaps a visit to the west coast, to explore some of those high class hotels. I would take my snorkelling gear so that I could come at them from the beach; all beaches are public in Barbados, so nobody could object. A long salt bath would probably be the making of me. Then later maybe head for the east coast again and explore those fabulous deserted beaches. It was the coast where the locals went to cure their ills; perhaps it would cure my hangover. Before I went in to shower, I looked over the patio wall and saw the feral cat searching the dustbins. I threw the last pieces of cake down for her.

THE FERAL CAT

Feral cat, the feral cat
Prowls about and fancy that.
Into the cane and out again,
Mouth full of rat and fancy that.

Feral cat, the feral cat
Neighbours garden and fancy that.
Scratches around and leaves a card,
All over the yard and fancy that.

When I awoke cat's face was there.
Belligerently I returned the stare.
Didn't see the leap, just fur in my face,
Sharp teeth in my neck, a warm embrace.

When I awoke, cat's face was gone.
I realised I was on my own.
A dream perhaps, a silly nightmare.
Then felt my neck and the bloody tear.

Feral cat, the feral cat
Night-time comes and fancy that.
Ballet step round sleeping dogs,
Starts a spat and fancy that.

Feral cat, the feral cat
Pretty creature and fancy that,
Midnight screams and daytime purrs,
Stealthy feline murderers-
                    FANCY THAT!

D. Stuart

parked the moke at the side of the road and walked through
to the beach. It was a little trek to Sandy Lane but I wanted
to take a look at this famous hotel and maybe I would spot
a star or two. This was such a pretty spot, the shoreline of the west
coast was all bays and calm seas. I adjusted the bag on my shoulder
and started walking.Several kayaks sped by and in the distance a
speed boat pulled a para sailor to incredible heights. I was so
engrossed that I nearly jumped out of my skin when a huge man
appeared out of the bushes, naked as the day he was born and
smiled at me. For a second I froze; this was one huge man and the
personal weapon he was pointing my way looked highly dangerous.
I ran the last stretch to the Sandy Lane Hotel beach where I
collapsed with my heavy bag and anxiously looked back. He was
gone.

There were so many parasols and loungers with hovering
waiters in attendance that I sheepishly laid my towel on the sand,
well away from them all. I thought, the beaches may be free but
there was more than a little subtle discouragement from fraternisation
with the wealthy ones. Later, I did swagger into the bar as though
I belonged there but one quick look at the prices sent me scuttling
off to the beach to pick up my things. I decided to leave the moke
where it was and walk as far as possible along the beach to the
other hotels. This decision had nothing whatsoever to do with not
wanting a second confrontation with the naked one. Right!

I found that beach erosion had brought the sea right up in
places and was forced to skirt around. Snorkelling was very
disappointing as all the coral seemed to have died which was
probably the reason for the seas coming in. I remembered the
clarity and wonderful coral in the Tobago Cays and wondered what
pollution had caused the destruction here. Perhaps it had something
to do with all the hotels and huge houses crowding shoulder to
shoulder on this west coast. Most of the properties were surrounded by high walls and fences which left little or no room for

locals to gain access to their 'free' beaches.

I stopped at the Colony Club and swam up to the bar for a drink. There was a steel band playing and my heart sank as I recognised the first notes of 'Beautiful, Beautiful Barbados' and wondered how long it would take to get the tune out of my mind this time. The atmosphere was very friendly and when I walked through the grounds afterwards, was fascinated by the way the water snaked around the apartments like an anaconda, so that many of them had their own "swimming pool" right outside their door. I continued my trek along the coast; by now the sand was so hot I had to walk in the breaking waves past Glitter Bay and the Royal Pavilion where the tanned and bejewelled bodies lined up toasting themselves. Several times I was approached by guys asking if I wanted to ski, jet ski or go out on a catamaran. I said no to all of them but then thought about it and went back to Tony with the catamaran. I was hot and getting tired; what nicer way to see the rest of the coast. I jumped aboard and lay down happily, letting Tony do all the work and thinking how much the life of the idle rich suited me.

It was amazing how much further you could intrude on the privacy of the rich and famous and their beautiful homes from the boat. Eventually we sailed into an inlet where Tony assured me I would find some good snorkelling. It was lovely, the beach was deserted and the sea life was much better if you swam a long way out to some coral gardens. Afterwards we found a shady spot under a tree where Tony produced some fish cutters and two beers. Soon I was dozing contentedly, 'Beautiful Barbados' playing insistently inside my head. I was vaguely aware of voices from the villa nearby. Tony said it sounded like a wedding party in progress. I couldn't be bothered to open my eyes and take a look.

SOMETHING OLD, SOMETHING NEW

The private jet taxied to a standstill at Grantley Adams and shortly afterwards a small group of people emerged; life members of 'The Rich and Famous Club' all geared up and ready for the Barbados season. Two large limousines awaited their arrival outside the customs area and the chauffeurs were soon settling their animated passengers inside. The mountain of luggage would follow.

Some thirty minutes later, the vehicles swept down a long driveway that wound through a small park and stopped at the imposing entrance of a Palladian mansion. Lord Charles got out with his fiancee Fiona and their guests and were greeted by the staff, lining the steps to the house. Fiona was a fun loving young girl who still couldn't imagine what it would be like to be called Lady Townshend after her marriage. She thought it made her sound so old, as old as her husband, and he was ancient! One of the secret grins that Charles found so intriguing about her, flashed across Fiona's face. Lord Charles had been honoured a few years earlier for services to the country, (millions donated to the Tory party), and was very particular that his title was used at all times. Fiona personally took the ladies upstairs to their suites while Lord Charles opened the first bottle of Bollinger for the men gathered in his den.

Leaving their guests to settle in and correctly deducing that everyone would be otherwise engaged for the time being, Fiona took the opportunity to slip into a bikini and crept out of the house. Keeping close to the trees, she by-passed the swimming pool and found the steps that led down to their own private little sandy cove. There are officially no private beaches in Barbados but this one was private, by virtue of the fact, that it was made impregnable from either side, by rocks jutting way out into the sea. Whipping off her top, Fiona dived into the water and started swimming hard. It felt divine; she had so longed for this in her fog bound London penthouse and with a strong lazy crawl she was soon just a dot in the distance. At last she tired and lay on her back, eyes closed, all tension gone. God how she loved this place.

Fiona reluctantly forced herself to return to her guests but as she neared the shore again she became aware of a familiar figure standing, waiting at the edge of the water; he was waving her bikini top in his hand. Yuk! That poxy little twerp Gerald; only son and sole heir, (until the wedding), to his father's (her future husband's), fortune. Otherwise referred to by friend and foe alike as, 'that little shit!'

"Give me my top Gerald! Immediately before I tell your father!" Fiona screamed at him as she emerged from the water clasping her hands over her breasts.

"What are you so shy about Fiona old love; I expect the world and his uncle have seen your tits; come on be a sport, give us a quick feel? I suppose a fuck's out of the question?" His smile, pure slime, slid over his face and brought down the corner of his mouth.

"Gerald, you little shit! If you don't give it to me immediately, I'm going to tell your father!"

"But that's all I want old love, 'to give it to you immediately'..."

"Master Gerald, your father is looking for you!"
The no nonsense voice belonged to Esther, the 'old retainer' as Gerald called her who had appeared on the steps and had been watching the whole performance. Gerald glared back at the old servant, as though he would defy her but then reluctantly dropped Fiona's top onto the sand, grinding it in with his heel before he turned and sidled away smirking.

"Thanks Esther, saved again. That little shit spoils everything." Fiona rinsed her top and Esther fastened it. Then they turned and hugged each other. She thought of Esther as her good friend; she also happened to be her maid. Esther had survived years of experience dealing with Gerald and although she had tried hard during that time she could never find a single attribute to commend him.

"I've known that good for nothing since he was a lad and he's always been a nasty piece of work.That boy's gonna be nothing but trouble for you Miss Fiona, you should be careful. He never takes his eyes off you and I wouldn't want you to get hurt.." Esther put a towel around Fiona's shoulders. The two women had enjoyed a special relationship right from the start, just one of those unaccountable things, having taken to each other the first time Lord Charles brought Fiona to Barbados six years previously.

"Don't worry Esther, I can handle that little shit with one hand tied behind my back." She smiled reassuringly.
The friends linked arms and went back up the steps to the house with their heads together chatting away like a couple of school girls. They would go over and over the arrangements for the wedding the following week. Fiona had brought the dress with her from New York when they had made a stop over on the way to Barbados, and she was delighted with her designer's work. The bridesmaids' dresses had already arrived from the U.K. The bride and her father would be taken to the church in a pretty buggy, drawn by a beautiful champagne blonde Haflinger and the ceremony would be conducted at St. James Parish Church, with a sumptuous feast afterwards, at The Royal Pavilion Hotel. Lord Charles had taken over most of the rooms there for the wedding guests; there were far too many to accommodate in the house.

Esther was very perturbed that as yet they did not have 'something old, something new, something borrowed or something blue.' Fiona said Esther was old fashioned and that sort of thing didn't matter any more. However, Esther looked stricken, so Fiona

98

assured her that they would find all the right things before the big day. It was part of Esther's charm that she still believed in old world courtesy and superstitions, and was firmly convinced one flouted these at one's peril.

The entire week before the ceremony was a social whirl with invitations to the residences of ambassadors and government ministers, as well as contemporaries, who also owned homes on the island, with Charles and Fiona giving wonderful dinner parties in return. Harpers and Tatler were specially invited from England to cover the wedding and they filled the social pages back home with famous partying faces and their equally famous designer clothes.

Gerald displeased his father at the first dinner by getting drunk and insulting the Chinese ambassador, so he was forbidden to attend any others. Gerald licked his wounds and as was his habit when his fury had no outlet, took his guns in the early hours to Graeme Hall swamp. There he killed and maimed as many birds as possible and as each fell earthward, he imagined it was his father dropping dead. It made him feel much better.

The wedding was a huge success and Fiona's Sloanie pals all assured her she looked better than a princess. The guests proceeded to celebrate in their normal outrageous fashion, getting horribly drunk and cavorting half naked, which gave the photographers a field day. They would sell the best photographs to the tabloids on their return. Nursing sore heads the next morning, the party-goers commiserated with each other and assured themselves that by the time they returned, London society would have forgotten their antics and the photographs; the paparazzi will have turned their poison dipped pens to some other poor bastards.

After a couple of weeks things began to settle down. Those guests who were not staying for the season went home and Fiona finally got used to being called 'Your Ladyship'.

A few more weeks passed uneventfully. Swimming, tennis, golf and the usual round of dinner parties. Then one evening loud voices were heard coming from the study. The staff said afterwards that Lord Charles was shouting at his son, insisting he return home to begin to work for him in one of his companies.

Lord Charles had apparently told his slacker of a son: "You'll start earning a living like it or not and you'll begin at the bottom as I did. You're obviously not fit for anything else! You couldn't even manage one bloody exam pass! I want you packed and gone by tomorrow!"

Gerald wasn't gone by the next day because at six a.m. the following morning the butler found Lord Charles slumped across his desk in a pool of blood. He had been killed by a single shot to the temple. A good looking police inspector arrived with some officers shortly afterwards. They spent some time questioning the family and staff and searching the rooms. Gerald, who was still asleep in his bed and befuddled with the previous night's alcohol, was rudely awakened and promptly arrested. In vain he pleaded his case to the Inspector; outstretched arms proclaimed his innocence but blood stained hands shouted guilty! Gerald stared in shock at his hands and screeched his innocence even louder but the murder weapon was found on his desk, blood spattered and with his fingerprints all over it. Gerald was carried off to Glendairy screaming to his new step-mother to 'get the best London lawyers out here immediately!'

Gerald had a lengthy wait in prison for the trial as criminal procedures do grind exceeding slow in Barbados, but he protested his innocence loudly every day. Everyone tut tutted and said, "It was bound to happen" and "I told you so".

It was a trying time for Fiona. First there was the funeral and then the court case. Gerald was eventually sentenced to life in a secure psychiatric hospital and was shipped home under guard to a nice place in Hertfordshire that resembled a country estate.

Esther said to Fiona at every opportunity, "I told you so," chupsed and carried on and on about not sticking to tradition. "You see, that's what brought all the bad luck. If only you'd had something old, something new, something borrowed and something blue, everything would have been all right. But you wouldn't listen to me!" Esther mumbled continually as she went about her work.

Fiona had that certain smile on her face as she mounted the stairs to her bedroom, trailing delicate fingers over the carved handrail. Thinking about it, she had stuck to tradition after all. That smile again. She raised her hand and counted off four fingers.

"One: something old? That would be Lord Charles. Two: something new? Herself. Three: something borrowed? Gerald's gun. Four: something blue?" She opened her bedroom door. "Well now, something blue. Ah yes." She glanced towards the police jacket lying on the chair near her bed and with a 'Whoopee!' landed right on top of the handsome inspector lying there, waiting for her.

The noise from the wedding party eventually woke me. I'd had a great time with Tony, who insisted on giving me a lift back to the moke. As we waited to cross the road, more wedding party guests were arriving. Stretch limos, several Mercedes and then a Rolls Royce passed in front of us and inside, a woman was waving frantically at me; she had several dogs on her lap and was laughing. I didn't know her from Adam but she obviously thought she knew me and I watched as the car drove through the gates with the lady still waving. Tony dropped me off and we arranged to meet the following night at The Boatyard. I decided I'd had enough of the west coast for one day and as hunger gripped me, I made up my mind to head for the wild solitude of the east coast and some reality. I took a different route this time which took me past St. Nicholas Abbey. Something about the place pulled me in but I resisted, promising myself that I would come back when there was more time and pushing onwards through an avenue of mahogany trees, soon came to Cherry Tree Hill. The panoramic view was outstanding and parking the car, I took several photographs of the landscape, the long white beaches and crashing tempestuous seas beyond, before reluctantly dragging myself back to the car. I drove slowly towards the coast road, past Morgan Lewis Mill on the right, then the cart road to Morgan Lewis beach which I had been told was lovely and deserted. Again, that would have to wait until next time. The wild Atlantic was now on my left; this was Cattlewash and I slowed to read the inscription on the 'Barclay Park' boulder. The beach after this was deserted, the wind fierce and the rock pools irresistible. I stopped the car and headed for the pools. The sand was burning so I sprinted over to the ocean and eased myself into the warm water, sending hundreds of crabs scuttling for deeper cover. In sheer luxury, I rested my head on a rock. From this level the seas looked huge as they crashed in but the little pool cocooned me. Never had I felt so at one with nature. There was not another soul about as I closed my eyes.

"Excuse me."

I nearly jumped out of my skin, I'd been half asleep. I sat up and looked around to put a shape to the voice.

"Look, I'm really sorry to disturb you. I didn't realise you were sleeping. Believe me I know how precious this place is when you want to be alone. Good bye, sorry again."

"No, please. I'm the one who should apologise. You just startled me. There's loads of room in here." I answered the cultured English voice. "My name's Duncan, by the way." I held out my hand. The man shook hands and stepped into the pool opposite me.

"I'm James, James Earl. I think I must have parked next to you up there." He nodded towards the road where a Suzuki jeep was alongside the moke, it had a surf board sticking out of it.

"You're surely not going to surf here?" I said.

James was tall, well over six feet and built like a rugby player. Easing himself down into the water he laughed.

"Not on your life! But I was not always so sensible."

He was a good looking man with short tousled hair blonded by the sun and humorous brown eyes. "This is my favourite spot you see. When the surfing's good I jump in the jeep and head for the big waves but I always stop here first. Superstition I suppose; for good luck. I really don't know what else to call it."

He looked at me. "Yes I do know, I'm just being shy. It's a homage you see."

"A homage. What to?"

"It's a long story. Are you sure you have the time?"

"I have nothing but time and I honestly cannot think of anything I would rather be doing right now. Please go on. I'm all ears."

James said that he was an author. Successful enough to spend three months of every English winter in Barbados. He owned a wooden bungalow up in the hills overlooking Bathsheba, where he found the quiet and bracing air, perfect for writing crime thrillers.

"But I must go back to the very beginning, to the first time I came to Barbados and totally fell in love with the island. I must have been about your age then."

JAMES EARL'S STORY

had only arrived on the island the day before and was already hopelessly in love with the place when I heard about the surfing at Bathsheba. I went out immediately and bought a long board, then headed for the east coast. It hadn't occurred to me that surfing would be good in the Caribbean, so my own board was safely tucked away in my Cornish home. The waves, apparently, were not giants like those in Hawaii, which I was very pleased about because I am no Laird Hamilton, who I'd had the privilege of watching once in Maui. As I approached the championships' venue, it was immediately obvious that parking anywhere near would be impossible. There were hoards of people about; I had never imagined there would be so many. Long lines of traffic were at a standstill, so I turned the jeep round and climbed up into the hills again, heading north. After a while, I turned right and once more found myself beside the water. Right here, in fact.

I stood on a low bluff, eyes sweeping the deserted beach below, taking deep breaths of sweet air into my smog filled lungs. I couldn't believe there was nobody about; I had all these beautiful waves to myself. A fresh breeze tugged at my hair and my ears were filled with the roar of Atlantic breakers, as they completed their long journey from Africa, far beyond the distant horizon. Gazing out over the cobalt water, I felt a sense of peace, an inner tranquillity that I had never found before in my travels. I decided there and then that I would make this spot a special place, my own private Eden.

The temperature was soaring as I walked onto the beach carrying my board and slowly I made my way towards the sea. I stood at the edge inspecting the water. There was a lot of rock about but I thought, if I could just paddle out to deeper waters it could probably be avoided. You see I just wanted to catch a couple of waves; I'd been so geared up for it and this way I wouldn't be disappointed. A feeling of lethargy was creeping over me and for a minute I was tempted to sink down on the sand and sleep. But the water was too inviting and felt cool as I lowered myself onto the board and started pulling my arms through the waves. I was out quite far very quickly and realised the tide must be turning as the waves were really building. Adrenalin tore through my veins as I sat up and waited for the big one to come. The wait wasn't long and there she was, a huge rolling, curling beauty coming towards me, shouting my name. I paddled hard to reach its speed. Then I was up, crouching, ready to answer the call. For one heady ecstatic moment I felt myself flying along the crest of the wave at great speed then suddenly I lost it and flipped over. The crash into the sea pushed the air from my lungs and I was soon swirling down, deep below the surface and gulping water, being turned over and over by a greater force than I had ever known. The incredible energy propelled me to the surface once again where I coughed water and took one small breath before I was dragged down again. Hurtled onto the coral, I was turned over and over and felt the skin flaying from my body. I tried desperately to hang on to the rocks but could feel myself losing consciousness as the relentless seas pounded over me until at last I had to release my grip. My body felt heavy. There was no longer any pain and my limbs hung like lifeless weights. I started to sink down and knew I was dying. Strangely I felt quite peaceful. My eyes were about to close when, through the water above, I saw this wonderful strong face and felt huge hands clasping me, lifting me up through the water as though I was weightless. Then I passed out.

When I woke up, I was terrified but calmed down as I felt the reassuring sand beneath me. A dreadful pain shot through my head and I felt disoriented. Slowly I looked around; the beach as before was deserted. It was then that I felt the pain, my skin was literally stripped from me in places and there were awful lacerations all over my body and legs; a small curl of seaweed draped over my left ankle. I coughed, tasting a vile salty wetness in my mouth, making me gag and bring up a lot of water. Rising unsteadily to my feet, I turned and made my way back to the jeep. If I tell you every step of the way was pure agony, believe me I do not lie. There was no sign anywhere of my surf board or the man who had saved my life. But I was determined to find him whatever it took. I would remember that face forever.

I managed to drive to a small wooden house, where the kind couple living there bathed and dressed my wounds, with something that, at last, brought some relief to the pain. They sent for an ambulance and while we waited they gave me green coconut water to drink and listened to my story in silence. I finished and after a while the old man spoke.

"As a young boy I was spellbound by the story of an Arawak Indian chief who was fishing with his beautiful young wife when their canoe capsized in a sudden storm. Despite his frantic efforts to save her, she drowned. It was at the exact spot where you got into trouble young man. Days later the Chief, in a state of inconsolable despair, paddled his canoe towards the setting sun. His people who were left on the beach, so the legend goes, heard the familiar voice of his young wife calling to him. He was never seen again."

"That's a wonderfully romantic story." I replied. "But I don't believe in ghosts and things. Anyway, how do you know my accident happened in exactly the same spot?"

The old man smiled knowingly to his wife and rocked his chair. "Go back to the same spot on the beach and look inland. You will see a row of palm trees, like sentinels standing guard. Look beyond them to the top of the hill and you will have your answer. There have been other incidents like yours and many people's lives have been saved."

After my release from the hospital, I drove straight back to the beach although I had been given strict orders to go home and rest for a few more days. I simply had to see for myself. My head was pounding, my body sore and aching but I just had to see.

As I stood on the beach, my back towards the ocean, looking inland, sure enough, there were the palm trees. And beyond? My gaze travelled upwards. A small sharply rising hill had over the years been riven by wind and rain into the perfect profile of a warrior's head. There was a sharply defined nose, a mouth which curled upwards at the edge and above the level of the eye, vegetation sprouted to form a headdress. I stared at the rocky outcrop which formed the chief's head. There was no mistake, I recognised the face. I'm not ashamed to admit that my cheeks were wet as I whispered, "Thank you chief."

I must have been looking at James transfixed because he smiled.
"So, Duncan, if you are a believer and find yourself on this east coast of Barbados where the sea is wild, take time to look just beyond the palm tree sentinel to that small sharply rising hill and say your hello to the Arawak chief."
James stood up and I was startled to see the scars that covered his body and legs. Then he turned and shouted at the top of his voice.
"Good morning chief, another wonderful day!"
His voice carried by the wind towards the hill and the ears of the sleeping warrior. He said that it didn't matter whether I believed him or not; he was past that. Most people thought he was crazy when he told the story so he stopped telling it eventually. A lot of the locals insisted it was just a children's tale, that adults should know better. But James Earl was a believer; there was still a sense

of magic in his life. Every time he came to this spot to be alone, sit on the beach and swim, he would greet the sculpture out loud and unashamed and would never forget to say good bye when he left.

"Did you just make that story up, Mr. James Earl, author?" I asked. James smiled resignedly.

"I told you, you wouldn't believe me."

"So where is this big chief carved out of rocks?"

"Look behind you, in the hills. Behind his sentinels or the row of palm trees."

I looked and sure enough, the shape of a head and headdress were clearly visible at the top of the hill, lying face up towards the sun. I looked back at James who was still smiling.

"James, I can really do without this sort of thing. Strange things have been happening to me since I arrived here which I've put down to raw emotions over my Mother dying" Noticing his cynical look, I added, "Also too much booze."
I went on to explain about my life in England, my mother's death, then coming out here and the weird things that had been happening to me since I arrived. I gave him some examples, like the constant sighting of King Dyall. The author then regarded me seriously.

'There are things in this world that we are taught from childhood not to believe in; we're told 'not to imagine things', that images we see and other people do not, therefore 'don't exist'. Do you realise how much research has been done on children who 'know' they have lived other lives, who can describe places they have never visited, speak a language unknown to their parents? Interestingly, they either 'lose' this memory of another time or stop mentioning what they know is reality by the age of four."
James gazed at the horizon.
"Some of us grown ups don't speak about the things we see either; fear of ridicule or whatever. Like the many sightings of U.F.O's by pilots, too worried about losing their jobs to report those sightings. But what if we all had these special powers long ago,

before we became 'civilised' for want of a better word?"

I was still trying to decide whether to take this strange man seriously.

"There was a time Duncan when we knew the value of life, gave thanks and honoured an animal that we had to kill for food. Now we are 'civilised'. We put them in pens where they can't even turn round. We feed them their own kind so that they become diseased and then we become diseased. We call this civilisation. We pollute the seas and kill majestic whales for cosmetics. We poison the land and more diseases are born; we bring proud beasts to extinction for their ivory; or make rugs from the skins of wonderful wild cats, or powder from rhino horns to make men more 'virile' so they can populate the world with more of this vile breed. We call this progress. We watch the holes in the ozone layer increase along with global warming; still we do nothing; too expensive, can't upset big business. Once, long ago, we felt the earth's breath, answered the call of the moon. We honoured our elderly; nurtured our young and spoke with the dead. Now all we honour is the almighty dollar and the plastic surgeon. We are ridiculous creatures Duncan and luckily I don't think we shall last much longer here. What goes around, comes around. We shall have our come-uppance. Nature will strike back and perhaps, in time, when the earth is purged, she will give birth to more worthy life forms."

James fell silent, looking out to sea. Then he laughed loudly, making me jump.

"Of course we won't be ready for it when it comes, we'll all be glued to the internet or T.V.! Seriously though Duncan, don't worry when you experience extraordinary things, rather celebrate. After all, you may just be realising a talent that belonged to us before everything started to go wrong."

We were both quiet for a long while, lost in our own thoughts.

"Well my friend, I don't know about you but I'm starving and I know just the place for us. Coming?"

What a strange man this James Earl was, one minute deep and mystical, the next ready for food and drink.

The Round House, which was just that, was perched precariously on top of a hill overlooking the eternal raging ocean. We had a marvellous meal there, talking incessantly while eating and drinking far too much. When we parted, we arranged to meet up the following week.

I kept to the highway for the trip back to the south coast, although it was tempting to take the slower route and pass by my little pink house. Next week end was Kadooment, the crop over festival I'd heard so much about. I was really looking forward to it. A whole crowd of us were going. Time was passing so quickly, I couldn't believe I had been in Barbados so long.

The next day I rose early. There were some things I needed in Bridgetown; five more films to be developed; yet another sketch pad and a note book. Wherever I went, I made notes; at every corner there was another picture to take and at every bar or cafe an interesting subject to sketch. I had a yen to add colour to my forms and by the time I left the shop, was well equipped with two small canvases, some brushes and a few tubes of oil paint. I went back for a folding easel and felt ridiculously pleased with myself. What with the snorkel and fins, my bag was getting heavier by the week to cart around. Crossing Fairchild Street, I looked for Kaylene (for some reason I had given the bag lady with the dogs this name). I was clutching my twenty dollar bill to give her but there was no sign of her or her dogs. I would have to be a bit more careful with my money in future but I wouldn't cut down on Kaylene's gift.

After taking the easel and paints back to the flat I had stopped to turn left onto the coast road when King Dyall cycled by. As usual he tipped his hat and without thinking, I wished him the customary "Good morning." The old gentleman looked at me and actually smiled, as though we shared a secret, before pedalling onwards. The car behind hooted in annoyance and I moved off round the corner quickly, hoping to catch the King but he was gone. There was no old man ahead of me riding a bike but then I hadn't expected there to be. And that was all right now.

Driving along past the airport and making my way to Crane Beech Hotel which I had first seen from the helicopter, the landscape had become noticeably flatter, more arid and less interesting. I parked the moke and entered the hotel where I had to buy an entry ticket, refundable with the first drink. It was well worth it. I walked past the swimming pool glancing up at the rooms on the right which must have had wonderful views of the surging seas. A dining room appeared on my left and there were chairs and tables outside, some of which were precariously perched on the high cliff ledge overlooking the long beach and turbulent seas. The view was amazing so I decided to have a drink first so that I could take it all in. The wind was fierce as I sat at one of the tables on the rock ledge. Steps had been cut into the cliff which led down to the beach. I watched a woman lose her hat to the wind and it was gobbled up by the churning seas below her. The beautiful uncrowded strand stretched out below while brown bodies rode the surf on boogie boards. I couldn't wait any longer to get down the steps and join the surfers. While I finished the drink, men started diving from the cliff into the boiling waters. I decided to give that one a miss. I spent a couple of hours body surfing; the undertow was deceivingly strong but it was exhilarating stuff. Afterwards, lazing on the beach, I felt so at peace with the world it would have been easy to stay all day but eventually, the thought of a cold beer pushed my tired legs up the everlasting steps, grown twice as steep since my trip down.

Back in the car, feeling tired but good, muscles stretched and toned by the surf, I made my way to Sam Lord's Castle. I liked the story of Sam Lord, who used to live there and made his money by enticing ships onto the rocks which he then plundered, murdered the crew and filled his coffers with the booty. When I arrived, however, I was disappointed. The place was teeming with tourists, so I changed my mind about lunching there and headed for my favourite east coast and the Atlantis Hotel.

I got lost only once. I was definitely improving. A sign came up pointing right for the Atlantis Hotel and I braked all the way down a very steep narrow road and parked. The place was tired looking but it had personality and I immediately loved it. The wind howled as I sat outside with a very good strong rum punch and looked down at Tent Bay, where the fishing boats rocked and rolled alarmingly. Soon a waiter appeared and asked what I wanted to eat.

"Fish or meat?"

So who needs menus? I thought. The food here was supposed to be great.

"I'll have fish please. Oh, and another rum punch."

I sat at a table overlooking the bay and the spray hit my face as I tucked into the hearty meal. There were three different types of fish – King Fish, Flying Fish and dolphin. Each one was succulent. There was sweet potato pie, okra and plantain to accompany the fish and the obligatory pot of hot sauce on the table. Afterwards, I had banana pie and coconut cream. The whole meal was delicious. They told me to be sure and come back for their Sunday buffet where I would be able to sample all the Bajan dishes. I would need no urging.

I called in on James Earl and we had a couple of drinks together, making a future date for Sunday lunch at Atlantis with a few mutual friends. Then I took the road home, past St Nicholas Abbey, which I still hadn't found time to visit and soon afterwards the air was filled with the sound of beautiful singing from a choir. I slowed as there were a lot of people surrounding the church; it must have been a special festivity. Turning onto the coast road I stopped beside my pink chattel house. It was still deserted, the lonely little rocking chair waiting patiently for its owner's return.

Crop over day arrived and I had arranged to meet my friends in the big tent on Spring Garden Highway. I couldn't get anywhere near there by car because of the hordes of people, so I parked and took off on foot. The place was a riot, masses swarmed the highway and there were stalls selling wonderful aromatic food everywhere. Loud speakers pounded music and drink tents were in abundance. I was just thinking I'd never find my friends when one of them called to me. He was dressed in a cowboy suit and said he was going to join a 'band'. The rest of the gang were in the tent and empty glasses already covered the table. The bands and the parade had apparently left the National Stadium early and were slowly making their way to the top of the Spring Garden Highway; some would not arrive until nightfall. We decided we had plenty of time to party before making our way along the highway to a high vantage point for a good look at the bands as they passed. I thought this must be the biggest street party I would ever go to.

People were already dancing on the road and I was told that the bands and the costumes would be spectacular. I was to look out specifically for the King and Queen of the Crop. All of a sudden, a hand reached out and pulled me to my feet to dance. I found I was facing a beautiful buxom lady who was gyrating her hips so provocatively that I didn't know what to do in response. She laughed, turned her back on me and clasped my hands around her waist. Her bottom was moving like it had life of its own against my pelvis and I found that I automatically had to move with her. Wukkin' up she called it. Simulated sex was more like it I thought. Boy, this was going to be one fun day!

SOMEONE TO WATCH OVER ME

Claudine had been up since dawn doing her chores and cooking her husband's breakfast. Now she was getting ready for church in her Sunday best. This Sunday was special as she had helped decorate the church for the festival and wanted to leave early to collect some flowers from her sister's garden on the way. Her sister Clarrisa, had given Claudine a lovely blue satin dress for this occasion, a dress which no longer fitted her because she had lost weight. Clarrisa had a good job in an office and owned her own car. She had started a walking regime with her husband and friends when they all got home in the evenings and what with her new diet, she was looking really good. Claudine had declined the offer to join their walks because there didn't seem enough hours in the day as it was, to do all her jobs. Besides, her husband Oliver was dead against it; said it was another example of "women getting out of their place." He and Clarrisa did not like each other. Clarrisa's husband helped with all the chores so they always had plenty of time to enjoy themselves.

Claudine looked at herself in the mirror and placed her white hat with the little blue flowers, on her head and swinging from side to side watched how the sunlight made her dress glow, like she was an angel. Oh! she clamped her hand to her mouth and looked over her shoulder as though the Lord was standing right there and had heard her, even though she hadn't voiced the thought. "Lord forgive me," she whispered.

Claudine tripped lightly down the stairs in her new dress; she was so happy with the way she looked for church. Clarrisa would be proud to stand beside her today. When Oliver saw his wife he hooted with laughter, "Jesus Christ woman, what de hell you look like. You'se too old and fat to dress so, you look like a whore. Go tek it off!"

Tears blinded Claudine's eyes as she went back to the bedroom to change. What if she'd gone to church looking cheap and everyone had stared at her and laughed? Oh the shame of it and in the house of God too. But then her sister wouldn't have given her something she would not look right in, would she? Besides, she couldn't help thinking that Oliver's outside women wore similar pretty clothes and he seemed to like those all right. But then she supposed they were so much younger.

Following several abortive attempts to leave the house, (Oliver always found extra things for her to do when he knew she was in a hurry), she eventually got away, rushing now because she was late. When she arrived at her sister's house, Clarrisa couldn't believe she wasn't wearing the dress and was furious. Not with Claudine, the gentlest of creatures but with the horror she had married. Taking her sister's hands in her own, she said, "He didn't like it eh?"

Seeing Claudine's eyes brim she hugged her and kissed her cheek. "You look really nice anyway Claudine."

Clarrisa calmed herself, then changed the subject. They began talking about the flowers they would pick to decorate the church.

While they gathered the blooms, Clarrisa broached the topic of divorce as she often did. Repeating for the umpteenth time that women were liberated creatures now, that they no longer had to put up with the ogres they had married, when they were too young to know any better. Her saintly sister would hear none of it, saying divorce was against the teachings of the church and that if she had this burden to bear, then it was God's will and that His designs would be made clear in time.

"Up there somewhere," she told her sister, "we all have a guardian angel who watches over us and sees everything we do. One day God will make His intentions known to me through that guardian angel."

Clarrisa felt so much love for Claudine; she had such a sweet child-like innocence, although she was a middle-aged woman. She hugged her and they walked on to church arm in arm.

Claudine always enjoyed church activities. Chatting to the people and singing with all her heart in praise of God with all the other voices always left her filled with a sense of peace and well being. On the way home, the sisters gossiped about the service, who was wearing what and giggled about Mrs. Bannister's loud off-key voice. At the crossroads, Claudine said goodbye to Clarrisa and hurried home. She had all Mr. Patel's dresses to finish before he called that evening to collect them. She was a good needle woman and Mr. Patel always had a lot of work for her. First though she must get her husband's meal.

Oliver was in a very bad mood when she returned. He had been reading the newspapers and several articles had displeased him. He told her that a woman was to be deputy prime minister and another one was to be minister of health. This latter had a fashionable shaven head which he made fun of and said that they were all wickers anyway. There had also been an article about 'Caribbean Men In Crisis'. The crisis was due, the reporter stated, to the success of women in schools, universities and the work place; saying that these women expected their husbands to share in housework, cooking and taking care of the children. The 'new women' would no longer put up with their husbands' outside women or 'deputies'. Claudine knew what was in the articles as she had already read them while Oliver was at work and she admired such women but they seemed a race apart from her. Oliver said the 'new women' were all married to queers and what they needed were real men to keep them in their places.

Claudine got to thinking and wondering about when it was that she had become such a nothing creature. Oliver was the only man she had ever known (in the biblical sense) and before him, she had been full of life and fun; she had loved to go dancing or to the beach. Trouble was, soon after they were married, her new husband began to change towards her. Little things at first, like ridiculing her at every opportunity; becoming critical of her walk, her cooking and the way she dressed. He derided her opinions and it wasn't long before she stopped voicing her ideas altogether. He even told her she had a terrible voice, and she so loved to sing.

Over the years his insidious carpings had led her to keep silent; it made for a more peaceful life. She stopped talking unless it was absolutely necessary, and apologised all the time automatically; although if you asked, she couldn't have said what she had done wrong. She even took to walking into any room where he was with a certain hesitancy, waiting for the verbal abuse. No matter how hard she tried to do things right, it seemed they never were right. Her all was never quite enough and his vitriol would always find a launching pad. It seemed strange to her that a man married a certain girl, presumably because he liked her; someone who was bright, full of life and love, then over the years turned her into something he detested. Then he looked elsewhere. Perhaps to someone who reminded him of that lost girl? As she became the woman of his making, he despised her more, but it was never more than she despised herself.

Claudine told herself she must not dwell on such thoughts; she was an ungrateful woman! Instead, she filled her head with her favourite hymn. One thing about singing silently, in the chapel of her head, was that she always reached the most perfect high notes. She smiled. The reverend said last Sunday that she had the voice of an angel. The smile slipped; he was probably just being kind. Oliver interrupted her thoughts by reading out that a little school-girl had been molested.

He said, "So much for women being equal!"
She looked at him; his face was mean. Was the boy she married

anywhere inside this man?

"Anyway," he went on, "if she's big enough, she's old enough. Those girls are prison bait, they go around asking for it!"

Claudine had to try really hard sometimes not to hate Oliver because she knew it was wrong. Humming louder in her head, she asked God's forgiveness for her thoughts. She knew that, with His help, her guardian angel would watch over her and never let things get too hard for her to bear. Oliver finished his meal and was watching one of the movies he got from under the counter, at the video shop, while Claudine tried to ignore what was happening on the screen and the movements in her husband's lap. Instead, she concentrated hard on sewing for Mr. Patel and songs filled her head.

In the afternoon, Oliver changed into his finery and told her he was going to the Crop Over festivities.

"I'm going to find some young big fat botsies to wuk up against! Not like yours old woman," he laughed.

Oliver told her he wouldn't be home that night or the next day, as it was a holiday and that he would be with his main squeeze if there was an emergency. Claudine watched him leave, saw him drive away in his shiny car and felt a huge relief. She could relax now. She was singing when Mr. Patel arrived and he said that she had the sweetest voice he'd ever heard.

"Like an angel's," he told her. She helped load his van with the clothes and put the money she'd earned into Oliver's drawer, then wearily climbed the stairs and slept like a baby until morning.

When Claudine awoke the following day, something felt different. It was very quiet, apart from the birds singing and even their song sounded mellow, sweeter somehow. The breeze through the window was cool and soft on her face, she felt....what? Well, she felt so relaxed, sort of heavy and such a feeling of contentment, dreamlike almost, yet there was an underlying edge as though something was about to happen.

She eventually dressed and went downstairs. It was as she

opened the kitchen window that she saw him. A beautiful angel! He was sitting against the well with his head resting on his arms. His delicate gossamer wings were folded down against his body and they glimmered in the morning sun as though they were made of gold. Was he a fallen angel? Was he hurt or just sleeping? Was he, perhaps, her angel?

She rushed into the garden and stared at the perfect vision before her. The angel had long locks that fell down his back and dark lashes swept his cheek as he slept like an innocent child. She watched fascinated as prisms of multi-coloured lights played out from his wings. So wondrous, so delicate that she felt something shift inside her; everything seemed unreal. Then she noticed that a pair of amber eyes were studying her.

With a gentle smile his full lips moved,

"Hello lovely lady."

Did he actually speak or did she just feel the words? She replied a tentative, "Hello." and asked if he was all right.

He said he was fine but, "...I was on a float that broke down at the carnival," which Claudine heard as, "When I was floating, something broke and I came down."

To which she responded in appropriate placatory fashion.

"Oh dear, not one of your wings I hope," she said with genuine concern. He jumped up, looked round at his wings and smoothed them with his hands. They were fine.

"I was in Lord Kitchener's good band," he continued, "and became so thirsty that I dropped into your garden for water and must have fallen asleep." Claudine heard this as, "I was in the good Lord's band" (of angels naturally); when I got very thirsty, I dropped down to your kitchen garden for water and fell asleep."

Claudine was amazed when he asked if he could take off his wings and put them in the shed for safe keeping. She didn't realise that angels could remove their wings.But thinking about it, it made sense as they would get in the way when they were going about the Lord's work, here on earth. Doorways would have been impossible.

She blushed as she realised she had been staring at what she could only call his white jock strap, (it probably had a heavenly name) but it seemed to be glowing as though it were covered with a thousand sequins. As he turned, she saw his buttocks were completely exposed. Of course he wasn't worried because he was an angel and bodies were very natural things, but Lord his body was truly magnificent. Huge hard muscles rippled as he moved and he moved so smoothly.

The Angel went into the kitchen, while she remained rooted to the spot and came back with two cups full of cold water. Into these he had placed some tiny flowers taken from a fold within the pouch and bade her drink. Never had she tasted water so sweet. They sat down on the grass and began to talk. He told her he was called Angelo (she thought he said 'Angel'), that his brother, who was called Gabriel (she knew that already) had flown with him from Havana. Claudine heard "... had flown with him from Heaven."

They spoke of many things and she told him all about her life, holding nothing back as God would probably have told him most of it already. They talked so easily together and he seemed interested in everything about her; but then he was her guardian angel after all. In a while, she asked if he would like something to eat but he said he would get something for her while she started sewing the new cloth Mr. Patel had brought.

Later he approached her and taking her hand away from the sewing, examined her needle scarred fingers and gently kissed each one, then raising her other hand, kissed the palm and where her pulse was beating at the wrist, let his full soft lips linger there. Angels certainly made you feel good. Helping Claudine to her feet, he said their food was ready.

Angel had made what he called angel hair pasta served with vegetables cut into tiny pieces that crunched as you bit into them. Some small angel cakes tasted spicy and were light as a feather. Afterwards, there was fruit which he insisted he feed into her mouth from his own. Claudine liked some of these heavenly customs. They finished with more flowered water and when she told him it was a divine meal, he smiled knowingly.

Angel took her to rest on the grass outside, in the shade of the trees. When he asked her to undo her buttons she did so; after all one shouldn't argue with an angel and when he removed all her clothes and they lay naked together, she still didn't argue. He stroked her body slowly and admiringly kissed every inch of her skin. Strangely, she was not at all embarrassed. When at last he truly took her to heaven, she was way past speech of any kind. Afterwards, he refused to let her dress because he wanted to 'watch her beautiful black skin as the waning sun's tongues of fire licked her soft curves.' She wondered idly if all angels spoke like that.

As Claudine looked with love and tenderness at the young face of her angel, she asked if he knew how old she was. He replied that time was man's invention and that he knew she was as old as the hills and newly born each day; just like him. He took her to heaven once more and she loudly called the name of the Lord for she was truly grateful. Later he helped her sew the garments before they slept.

In the morning, he kissed her eyes awake and explained he had to leave for a while but would be back to collect her by mid-day. He noticed her concerned look and smilingly said not to worry; she had someone to watch over her now.

Angelo was back by noon as promised. He said they were to leave to do God's work in the Garden of Eden, that they would love each other always and be together until God called them. Angelo had actually said he loved her and that he had found work as a gardener on a big estate called Eden Lodge. They could live together in a small wooden house in the grounds for as long as he did the gardening.

He presented her with two beautifully wrapped packages, (obtained with money he'd found in a drawer upstairs) and a single red rose from the Garden of Eden. She undid her presents with the awe of a child and found herself holding what he called a Teddy;

a white flimsy affair which delighted her and which he said he wanted her to wear for him that night, which made her giggle. The other parcel contained a small book of poetry which he said they would read in the evenings, when their day's work was done, and after he had taken her to heaven and they held each other close. Claudine inhaled deeply, enjoying the heady perfume of the red rose which he had taken from Eden Lodge and knew that all she had endured with Oliver had been worth while, to be rewarded with such incredible happiness now.

Later, there were several stares as the strangely dressed couple, obviously in love, made their way hand in hand through the streets to Eden Lodge.

As for Oliver, he arrived home the following evening to find an empty house and a note addressed to him on the table. It read...

'The Angel came to take me to Heaven. I gone.'

Many years later in his lonely old age, Oliver would remember Claudine, not Claudine the 'frump' as he used to refer to her but strangely enough he always saw her as the young girl he had married. He had finally concluded that she had lost her mind and gone off somewhere. One thing though; he'd never been able to explain the wings he'd found in the old shed. Naturally, he never told anyone about them. They would think he'd gone mad too!

My splitting headache had lasted all day, prodded incessantly by misty memories; jumbled scenes of yesterday's Kadooment fever flashed across my mind. I remembered that during the fabulous parade, I had been pulled up onto one of the trucks decorated in the style of a desert prince's tent. In front of us, moving slowly because they were being swamped by females, was a band of angels. They were all handsome males with body builder physiques, clad only in white sequined jock straps with diaphanous wings strapped to their backs. I remembered the sea of laughing faces beneath me and could recall belly dancing with some very sexy mermaids with two tiny shells covering their nipples and I still can't imagine how they remained stuck on! Other than that, I remember nothing. I awoke the following day on Brandons Beach. Next to me, still asleep, was a Rastafarian with long dreadlocks. My own hair, I discovered when I touched my head delicately, had been braided and had little beads in it. I also seemed to have acquired a black tee shirt with a lion's head on the front and the word 'Jah!' underneath. I knew that, as usual, a salt bath was the only answer. Hesitantly I tried to stand, my head felt twice its normal size and was full of cement. Then I was violently sick. Still I made my way to the sea and struck out in a slow crawl, the cool salt water felt wonderful and I was soon feeling more human.

Here I am now, a day later and still feeling delicate. The awful thing is a friend has just called to remind me that we are doing a club crawl this evening, starting in St. James and finishing back on the south coast where we all lived. I must make myself some boiled eggs with soldiers and drink a large glass of milk, my mum's cure all for any ailment. Funny, I am getting used to being able to think of her without feeling that awful wrenching cramp in my chest. Now I am filled with good memories and realise what a waste it is being sad about loved ones–almost an insult to the happiness they gave us while they were alive.

I was feeling practically normal by the time I picked up two of my friends and headed for St. James and was soon caught up in their party mood. We were turning right past The Pelican Village when I saw my old friend Sarah, who had sat next to me on the flight from Gatwick. She was sitting at the back of a taxi with her husband, waiting to turn into the port. I shouted to her; she turned and beamed in instant recognition and was winding down her window to speak when her husband ushered the driver on. She continued waving to me out of the back window until the taxi disappeared. I had telephoned Sarah several times but there was never an answer. The last time I tried, her husband had picked up

The Angel

the receiver. I left a message for her with the address and telephone number of the flat but had the strongest feeling that she would never receive it. I'd always hoped to bump into Sarah somewhere on my travels. After all it was such a small island but it was not to be. Never mind, she looked happy enough. Maybe the miserable bastard was taking her on holiday!

TWO'S COMPANY

Roger stretched out on the settee, replete from the evening meal and ready to watch T.V. until bedtime. He could hear Sarah washing up in the kitchen humming a tune.

"Shut up will you Sarah, I'm trying to watch the news, you've had all bloody day to sing!"

After a hard day working at his off-shore company he expected a little peace and quiet. Well it hadn't been all day exactly. After lunch at Sandy Lane with Gina, they'd spent most of the afternoon at her flat having wild sex. Boy these island women were hot stuff! They just couldn't get enough and everyone knew they had the special hots for white men. His thoughts had started a stirring in his underpants and he reached down to adjust himself, leaving his belt and zip undone. All those meals out with Gina as well as Sarah's home cooking were really putting on the pounds. But hey! when you're hot, you're hot and Gina said his frame could take it. Roger belched loudly.

Sarah finished her chores and came into the room. She had no make-up on and her face was wet with perspiration.

"God it's hot."

She wiped her forehead and neck with a flannel. "I'll never get used to this heat; the summers seem to get worse every year."

She flopped down beside her husband. He glanced at her with undisguised disgust. Well if anything could deflate his old boy it was good old Sarah.

"It doesn't help that you've got so fat. You should go on a diet."

Roger mumbled without taking his eyes off the screen. She had not adapted well to their move to the Caribbean. Where was the slim, fun filled little blonde that he'd married twenty years ago. No wonder men went off the rails when their women let themselves go like that. He raised his backside and farted.

"Cor, that's better out than in!"

Sarah moved away and studied him from the armchair.

"It's all right for you. You have an air conditioned car to take you to your air conditioned office. By the time you get home at night it's a lot cooler. If I had a car I could get a job or visit with some friends or..."

"Do shut up Sarah, you're like an old gramophone record, moaning on and on. I've told you when we can afford it I will get you a car. As for friends, you haven't got any you silly old mare."

Sarah stared at him, "Perhaps if I could get out more I would find some. Since we got back from England four months ago I've really felt the loss of my mother. I need a friend..."

"Yeah, yeah, yeah."

Truth was it wouldn't be convenient for Sarah to be able to move about. She might see things she shouldn't! Anyway he really couldn't afford it. Gina was costing him a fortune, what with the flat he rented for her and the new car. Shit though, she looked so good in that red sporty Miata, a real crumpet car if ever there was one.

When Gina first came up with the cruise idea, he was dead against it and immediately said no, that it was totally out of the question. But Gina was never one to take no for an answer. He insisted that they couldn't possibly get away with it. But she was a bright girl and suggested that he take Sarah along too. At first he thought it was a crazy idea. Then Gina explained as she slowly walked over to him, hips swaying seductively, wearing only a thong, that she would stay in a nearby cabin. Gina wet her lips and climbed onto his lap, teasing him with her breasts and moving against him until he was hard.

"Please big man; imagine coming to my cabin whenever you want; imagine what I would do to you."

She unzipped his pants, brought her lips to him, then stopped and stood up. "Yes or no big boy?"

"Yes, yes, yes but please please go on!" he pleaded, pushing her head back down.

As Roger lay there afterwards, Gina's idea appealed to him more and more. He laughed and said, "It brings new meaning to the expression 'two's company, three's a crowd'!"

What a girl Gina was. It would also shut the old bag Sarah up for a while. He reluctantly brought his thoughts back to the present and adjusted his crotch again.

"Go and make us a nice pot of tea Sarah girl."

She got up reluctantly and as she walked towards the kitchen, he shouted after her.

"At least you have your volunteer work at the hospital, and don't I always drop you off and pick you up again?" She soon returned with the tea tray.

Roger said, "Anyway, I have a nice surprise for you. Go over to my desk and bring me that folder. We're going on a cruise round the islands."

Sarah's mouth dropped open.

"You're serious, you mean it? This is not one of your jokes Roger?"

"No I'm serious, we're going on the Free Spirit, that computerised sail ship we see in the harbour every Saturday. Here's our itinerary."

He flung the brochure at her.

"We're leaving in ten days so you'd better get yourself a couple of nice outfits. I don't want you letting me down on the ship. We could meet some useful people."

With the money Roger gave her, Sarah bought a couple of dresses, a long black skirt and matching top, which she thought was quite slimming plus a caftan to go over her swimsuit and there was still a bit left, to treat her children at the hospital to some goodies.

Sarah worked with special children at the clinic and she loved it. It was there that Sarah, the earth mother, could give full reign to her nurturing nature. The response of the little ones was always so real. Some weeks previously, she had invested in paint boxes and paper and had started to teach those who could manage a brush to paint. Some held the brushes in their hands. If they didn't have the use of their hands they used their toes and if they had neither, their mouths. Sarah's heart swelled with pride looking at her little children. She told them that she wouldn't see them the following week as she was going on a big boat. So they all decided to paint the boat, the sea and Sarah in the waves. Some pictures were really quite good and others sent them all into fits of laughter.

The child Sarah worried about most was little Chantelle, the daughter of a single mother. The little girl could do very little for herself as they did not have the facilities of the more wealthy countries to aid her. So Sarah carried her around all the time on her hip, showing her everything, talking to her and making jokes. There was no response from the child but Sarah kept on trying. Her young mother loved her, and came to the hospital as much as she could but did not have the money to take the child abroad, for the specialised treatment she needed. Sarah asked a friend, who worked with her at the hospital, to pay special attention to Chantelle while she was away as the girl was very dear to her.

At last Saturday came and Sarah and Roger arrived at the port. What a surprise seeing Duncan Stuart in that moke with the other lads. He certainly looked happy though and had she seen beads in his hair? Bit of a change from the sad, lonely boy she had met on the plane. Sarah felt ridiculously pleased that he seemed to be having fun but more than a little disappointed that he hadn't got in touch with her. Thinking he may have lost her number, Sarah had eventually telephoned his hotel, only to be told that he had left and was renting a flat. Maybe seeing her would jog his memory, he seemed to be different, more sensitive than most men Sarah had come across.

Having paid the taxi driver, they walked behind the porter who loaded their bags onto a trolley and pushed it towards the ship. Free Spirit was beautiful and Sarah gazed up in awe as they walked alongside. The porter put the bags onto a conveyor belt and they climbed the gangway to the deck, where the Captain was waiting to greet them. They were then guided into a lounge where rum punches and nibbles were served while boarding formalities were completed.

Sarah couldn't remember when she had felt so happy. There was a time of course, way back in her childhood years, spoilt by loving parents and brought up in a happy stable family. She was happy then, thought the world was a big exciting place, full of nice happy people like herself. Then she left home and got married. Roger had been very good looking when he was young. She had never had a boy friend before and her parents said he was a good catch. Sarah was bright, pretty and talented. Her music and art teachers thought she was good enough for a career in either subject but everything had to be put on hold when, so young, she fell in love. His career was paramount and she willingly and enthusiastically devoted all her vigour to being the perfect business man's wife. She always thought that she would be able to continue her studies once Roger was established and indeed, he promised as much. In those early days though, he said he needed her to be the perfect social wife, to impress his bosses with sophisticated dinner parties and cocktail gatherings. Once the marriage and his career were established, Roger's promise to let her return to college became null and void; he had other ideas. He told her continually how much he loved her, couldn't bear for her to be away from his side for a moment and Sarah was flattered. He needed her undivided attention, didn't that show how dear she was to him? Then he really shocked her by confessing that he didn't want children and actually cried as he explained why. He said babies would demand all her love and she would have none left for him.

It was for the same reasons he discouraged friends or outings unless it was a short, mundane and necessary trip to the supermarket. She held her husband, comforted him and reassured him that he would never have to share her with anyone. In the beginning, she believed that she was precious to him and endured the sulks and long silences, whenever he didn't get his own way. When she finally got over the feelings of the walls closing in on her, and being trapped, she began to feel the comfort of them and became almost afraid to go out.

Then the dinner parties for Roger's business associates started being an agony for Sarah, as his humour became directed at her, often to the enjoyment of his guests. In the end, she became so clumsy and unsure of herself that he started taking his business associates out to restaurants instead. She no longer recognised the woman she had become and he no longer bothered to hide the philanderer he had become. The fact that he despised her was clear in his eyes but it was nothing to the extent she despised herself.

She thought their move to the Caribbean would change things. How wrong she had been. She caught herself gazing wistfully at an older couple, standing with their arms around each other, drinking their rum punches and laughing at secret jokes. If only life could be like that for everyone. Come on Sarah, she chided herself, this trip will be the dawning of a new age. She downed her drink and whisked another from the waiter's tray as her husband chatted to the purser.

Their cabin was lovely. There was a large double bed with a television overhead, a dressing table, loads of cupboard space and a nice bathroom. She ate some of the grapes that topped the welcoming fruit bowl and told Roger she was going to luxuriate in the shower. He told her that he was showering first as he had things to do, so she lay on the bed contentedly until he came out of the bathroom. As she watched her husband dress, Sarah tried hard to suppress a giggle when his face reddened with the exertion of fastening a collar, made too tight by his excessive eating. He told her he was going to have a look round the ship and would see her later in the bar. "If we miss each other for any reason, I'll find you at dinner." Sarah was pleased to be left alone; she didn't want any criticisms spoiling her mood.

After her shower she used some body cream from a bottle on the shelf that smelt divine and she looked at herself naked in the mirror. Wild, unruly blonde hair had curled in the shower and fell in tight little waves, that would need fastening back, to comply with the way Roger liked her to wear it. The Caribbean sun had lifted the colour with streaks of white blonde, interspersed she noticed with the odd grey hair. Sarah straightened and examined her figure. She had that creamy white skin, the type which never tanned, only burned, so she stayed in the shade or liberally coated herself with factor thirty before going in the sun.

When they were first married, Roger said he loved her skin. Now when she got into a swimsuit, he told her she looked like a beached whale. She certainly had put on some weight, thanks to comfort eating. Sarah climbed into her long black skirt and pulled a black ribbed top over her head. Smudging a blue kohl pencil into the outside corners of her eyes (the lady at Harrisons had told her it enhanced their darkness), she smoothed coral lipstick on her full lips and stood back to study herself. Sarah giggled. She actually giggled out loud! It must be those rum punches and she felt a tingle of excitement as she slipped into her shoes and opened the cabin door. Then she glanced back at herself in the mirror, tore the combs from her hair and shook the curls free around her face. She left the cabin feeling like a naughty girl and still grinning, made for the bar.

Meanwhile Roger had found the cabin of the temptress, Gina and had lost no time in jumping on top of her. Roger didn't believe in preliminaries and he wanted his money's worth on this trip; he had paid a lot for this cruise after all. What he liked about Gina was that no foreplay was necessary, not like those modern bitches

in England. The last one he shagged had told him he was strictly a whip it in, whip it out and wipe it merchant. She'd said that he should save countless women from years of torment by using his hand! Cold bitch what did she know? Probably a dyke anyway. God, Gina was coming already and he'd only just gone in; what a woman!

"Roger, sweets, you are one hot man, I never had it so good, you drive me crazy. Tell me truthfully, are all Englishmen this good?"

"I always say Gina, you've either got it or you haven't. You are one lucky girl and I'm all yours."

"Shouldn't you be getting back to Sarah; we don't want to spoil things."

"You're right. You know what I love about you is that we're two of a kind. We have a lust for living and loving and to hell with everyone else, right?"

"You said it big man. Will I see you after dinner?"

"You betcha. After a couple of glasses of wine Sarah passes out for the night. As soon as she's snoring I'll come back."

When Roger got to the bar he couldn't see his wife at first, then he spotted her standing in the middle of a small group of people, drinking and laughing. He hardly recognised her. What on earth had she done to her hair? Walking quickly over, he introduced himself to the group, immediately taking over the conversation, to make up for the inanities his wife had obviously been spouting. A tall Italian with glasses said how very disappointed he was at the sight of Roger; that he thought Sarah was single and might keep him company for the entire voyage. Then he took her hand and kissed it. Roger grabbed Sarah's arm just above the elbow so tightly that an angry bruise would surface later.

"Sorry, but we're late for dinner and with a body like Sarah's you have to fill it up regularly or she deflates like a blimp!" Roger roared with laughter at his joke but nobody else joined in and they seemed genuinely sorry to see her go.

"That's the trouble with Yanks and Ities, no sense of humour."

Roger said as he steered his wife to the dining room. Sarah had been having a wonderful time with those interesting people; they were so friendly and really seemed to like her and find her amusing; the rums of course had helped loosen her inhibitions. Roger's intrusion and then his awful patronising joke had brought tears to her eyes. She thought she'd grown immune to his jibes over the years but tonight it hurt, probably because she was enjoying herself so much. She'd felt that she looked really attractive, had made friends with perfect strangers and everything was right with the world. Then those few words from her husband had deflated her like a balloon, like the blimp he called her. She felt humiliated, insignificant. Why had she let him get to her tonight of all nights?

Quickly brushing her lashes, she responded to a good evening from the maitre'd, who asked if they would like to dine alone or share a table. Roger decided they would like company and they were taken to a table where a very distinguished looking middle-aged American couple were sitting. They all smiled and introduced themselves. Sam was a doctor and his wife Jane, a lawyer. Roger was immediately impressed and called the waiter to order champagne. Their dining companions declined Roger's offer to share the champagne, thanking him but explaining that it would not go with the food they had ordered and that they would stick to the red already opened; adding that they would be only too pleased to share this with Sarah and Roger.

The meal was superb. Sarah went through every course on the menu and drank half the bottle of champagne too, studiously ignoring Roger's meaningful looks each time the waiter re-filled her glass. She listened intently to the fascinating couple's tales of their work and their travels. Roger, on the other hand didn't really seem to be having fun. After several crude jokes that seemed to embarrass rather than amuse, there was a ridiculous altercation with the waiter, when Roger sent back his carpaccio because it wasn't cooked properly. After a brief moment, when everyone tried desperately to stifle laughs, they all erupted simultaneously, including the waiters. Roger set his lips and went into a deep sulk, only rousing himself to replenish his glass with the couple's wine. This incident set the tone for the rest of the meal for Roger, and immediately after dessert, he pulled Sarah to her feet. "It's time for bed; you may have noticed that my wife can't really handle too much booze."

In truth she was more than a little tiddly and waved happily to her friends as they left the dining room.

Much later that night, to the sound of Sarah's snoring, Roger crept quietly out of the cabin and along to Gina's room. She was already waiting for him, lying naked on the bed while soft candle light flickered round the room. Roger stripped off, smelt his arm pits, shrugged and leapt aboard. But in spite of Gina's expert attention, for the duration of a lengthy amount of time, he simply could not rise to the occasion. Roger blamed Gina. She was wrong to be lying naked on the bed; this put him immediately under intolerable pressure and the thought occurred to him that perhaps she was losing her touch. It may be time to get a new model. He would think about it in the morning when he could think straight. Gina tactfully suggested a stroll on deck to clear his head and he agreed. They kept to the dark areas in case they were recognised but Gina soon got fed up with his sour mood, told him so and said she was going to bed. He was left on deck to sulk alone.

Good riddance, Roger thought as she opened the door and disappeared inside sending a blast of freezing cold air at him. He stood by the rail thinking of those pratts at dinner; the blob he was married to and Gina's replacement. It was pitch black and the stars were bitter bright watchful eyes. He'd certainly had a skin full tonight and eaten far too much food. He felt bloated and in pain. He levered himself against the rail and raising his left leg did the loudest, longest fart of his long career in the art. He was bemusedly congratulating himself when, without warning, he was up-ended. Roger was so surprised to find himself actually flying through the air, that his mouth was still open in amazement, as he hit the water far below and the scream that finally came sank with him. It made drowning that much easier. The stars twinkled in the blackness and everybody it seemed was sleeping, apart from the bridge of course and a night stalker or two.

Sarah raised the alarm, as soon as she got up the next day and noticed the still fluffed up pillow on the bed next to her. The captain and crew were very sympathetic, turning the ship immediately and retracing its course. Notification was signalled to all vessels in the area but as expected, there was no sign of Roger. After due consideration, Sarah decided to stay with the ship until it returned to Barbados, explaining to the captain that she couldn't possibly face having to traverse the small airports on an island hop home.

The other passengers were wonderful, so kind and caring whenever she took her book up onto the deck. Sarah got her thoughts in order and planned her future, as she lay soaking up the bracing sea air or watched the dolphins dive and leap with glee in the ship's bow wave. There was plenty of time to think. She would sell everything as quickly as possible and return to the cool air and pastel shades of her beloved England. She took all her meals in the privacy of her cabin and every day she felt stronger. A force was growing inside her that said, "You are Sarah, a unique wonderful woman; healthy in body and agile of mind. You are alive and there is so much living to do."

Sarah had showered and was rubbing the sweet smelling cream over her body when she heard a light tapping. Placing a towel round herself she opened the cabin door. A huge grin split her face when she saw that it wasn't the cabin boy. At last her lover had come to her. Their eyes locked, the door was pushed shut and the towel was tugged away. Her lover loosened the tied hair so that it spilled around her face; and reminded her that she never, ever had to tie it back again.

The dark eyes of her loved one were filled with a desperate

yearning as they began a slow journey over Sarah's body, lingering with such a hunger that Sarah felt herself go weak at the knees. She felt desirable and beautiful. Then those magic hands were softly caressing her breasts, the demanding mouth nibbled, kissed and sucked with murmurs of love and pure delight at the softness found there and marvelled at the whiteness and size. Slowly the caresses moved downwards; at first like the downy wings of a thousand birds then becoming more intense, exciting every nerve ending in Sarah's entire body until reaching her secret places and turning Sara's legs to jelly, the two lovers collapsed onto the floor.

A long while afterwards Sarah sighed contentedly, opened her eyes and whispered.

"Darling we did it! We really did it, didn't we?"

"Yes my love, we did. You are free to be the beautiful person you are. I love you so dearly Sarah."

"I love you too Gina," Sarah whispered back.

For the last couple of weeks I had been really living it up. All my friends knew that I was booked on the Wednesday flight back to England and every one of them had determined to give me a send off, Caribbean style, which meant a party every night. Some days I barely caught more than a nap before it was time to get ready for the next big event. If I lived here I would be an old man before I reached forty.

Last night had been no exception; a big house party first and then we headed for the clubs, finishing at Harbour Lights where, after doing something called The Donkey, I had apparently passed out cold. The cat woke me, scratching at the refuse bins. My head hurt worse than ever before, I daren't even move my eyes. Eventually hallucinations of tall glasses filled with freshly squeezed orange juice and ice brought so much torment that I made a move. Slowly, gently, like a bent old man I made my way to the fridge and gulped down two tall glasses of juice. I splashed my face in icy cold water until I started to feel better; then I had to rush to the toilet where I brought it all back. I thought it was a good thing that I was going home on Wednesday, I could never survive out here but conversely the thought of actually going home brought such an intense sadness, that I sat down and tried to analyse my feelings. Was this what they called Boozers Gloom? I had certainly packed more living into the last months than I had in my entire life. I couldn't even remember how many, well let's call them 'liaisons' I'd had; sometimes I couldn't even remember the name of the girl I woke up with. But was that fair? Was what I had been doing really living? There were times lately when I had the feeling that the real me was standing in the sidelines watching the 'new' me. I understood that I'd been making up for lost time, for all the sad quiet years looking after my folks. But even that wasn't fair because that's like discounting a childhood full of laughter and happiness before my father's illness. And my dear Mum, ever ready with a smile for me right 'til the end. The way we used to pour over the old photographs from the chest, the Barbados connection that sent me out here in the first place, and still I'd made no effort to find any records. Well I had two days left and they would be spent in pursuit of my long lost ancestor. No more parties! I showered and made an omelette which I sat and ate, while I thumbed through my collection of sketch pads and writings. I had started my diary of events in the first person. A section titled, 'First Impressions' began...

My name Is Duncan Stuart and I have come to Barbados to research my ancestry. Somewhere along the line, way back it seemed, my family had lived here for some fifty years. On arrival, I was totally unprepared for the sheer beauty of the place. Everything was just too much; the sky an impossible blue, the sea a deep cobalt through to the softest shades of aquamarine and veridian. From the jumbo, I saw coves and stretches of white sandy beaches and on the drive from the airport to my hotel, the bright colours of the tropical flowers were set off by a greenery so intense and bright it hurt my eyes. I immediately found the people friendly and smiling. The atmosphere was soporific and I decided all I wanted was to sit in the sun and soak up all the new sensations. Bugger the research!

So for a few days, I made like a typical tourist and was soon feeling tanned and rested. I bought a sketch pad and already have a collection of drawings—scenes that had caught my eye; like old St. Hill sitting, staring into her glass full of rum; the cricket match where the excellent bowler had a plaster on his bald pate; a typical chattel house with a rocker on the stoop. There was one of a beautiful girl coming out of the water in just a thong while a man waved a bikini top at her. Another showed a reveller dressed as an angel from the Kadooment festival and I had even sketched scenes from a couple of awful nightmares that had woken me.

I hired a mini moke, then decided on an early morning helicopter tour of the island, just to get my bearings, and was very glad I did. From the air you could see the vast differences in the coastlines; we started south where the sea was choppy and people were playing in the waves, the water was scattered with the multi-coloured bright sails of wind surfers; our pilot said the championships were on at Silver Sands, something I should not miss. Flying on, we passed Crane Beach Hotel perched on top of a cliff with a white sandy beach below. Here the waves were bigger and littered with boogie board riders. Then it was Sam Lord's Castle, named after the legendary pirate who had lured ships onto the reef, so that his men could plunder their cargo. Soon opening up before us was the wild east coast of the island with stunning long beaches, many of which seemed deserted. Here the long boards were out and surfers were riding the big rollers. Finally, we reached the tranquillity of the west coast, or as the pilot called it, millionaire's playground. What an incredible island this is.

I had apparently not liked this beginning as it had been crossed out and I had started again but at Gatwick Airport. All this seemed so very long ago and there were many incidents written down that I have entirely forgotten about, sketches I couldn't remember doing. Was I really that drunk? Leafing through the pages I found a couple of poems and thought 'Pam Ayres eat your heart out!' I noticed though that my notes became less and less, more rushed, careless. It was easy to see where party time had taken over. All this whetted my appetite for a proper effort in the search of my ancestry, just as Mum and I had planned. I put my book, sketch pad and camera into my bag and started walking to my moke which I had prudently left parked by the Careenage some time during last night's festivities.

MIRIAM

I crossed the bridge over the Careenage, where the buildings were reflected in the water's early morning light and thought how Wayne Branch's paintings had captured the scene, so perfectly. As I walked towards the car park and my moke, a lovely local girl in a flowing white cotton dress was sitting on the wharf, legs dangling over the side; she was gazing out to sea. She turned as I drew nearer and catching sight of me broke into a huge grin. "You're late Duncan Stuart," she called, "but I knew you would come."

I was really embarrassed as the girl looked vaguely familiar. Had we met at The Boatyard last night and made a date? I honestly couldn't remember, but then I'd been stoned out of my mind. Still she was very pretty.

"Hello," I answered.

I told her that I was touring the island and asked her to be my guide which made her chuckle. It was the sort of deep chuckle that made you join in for no reason. Suddenly I felt so happy I wanted to shout it to the world. She pulled a small hat made from palm fronds onto her head and smiled at me.

"You know what Mummy always says Duncan. Protect your skin Miriam, always wear a hat!"

At least I knew her name was Miriam. We drove north, out of the parish of St. Michael, chatting about everything, her arms entwined with mine, her head resting on my shoulder, which made driving a bit dodgy but I was enjoying the sensation too much to pull away.

Miriam

Soon we entered St. James, past the expensive hotels and houses which she ignored as we passed, seeming to have eyes only for me. It was very flattering and what's more it seemed genuine. I'd seen too much of the false variety over the last few months so I'd become an expert. Eventually we arrived at a beach bar, where we stopped for a cooling drink of coconut water. Miriam and I never seemed to stop talking as we strolled along the sand letting the water lap at our toes, my arm resting easily around her. Returning to the moke I studied the map, then we set off again through St. Peter heading for St. Lucy.

Driving through Speightstown, we passed the new Marina development, then on to Six Men's Village and cross country until we saw a sign to Mile And A Quarter. I smiled, once more delighting in the names of the villages, made even more poignant by having Miriam along. I was ridiculously happy to have her by my side, sharing experiences together, someone to say 'Wow, look at that!' to. A couple of times I insisted on going down a little lane, marked on the map but each time we found the road petered out to nothing, which Miriam thought was hilarious and said, "I told you so."

We parked at North Point, Miriam's favourite place and stood on the top of a bluff where the Atlantic pounds the cliffs. Entranced by the panorama before us, we stood letting the wind whip our faces bringing a crazy elation. We held hands and walked down the steps to the Animal Flower Cave.
I said disappointedly, "But Miriam, where have all the flowers gone?"
She laughed again, "Dear Duncan, long gone, long, long gone."
Racing towards the cave opening high above the raging sea, she stood arms outstretched, a dark silhouette calling to the turbulence below. It looked as though she was going to dive and for a second, with the blinding sun behind and the white of her dress, I lost her and screamed her name. A terrible, unreasonable fear took hold of me that she had fallen but then a light touch on my arm assured

me she was beside me again.

"Don't do that again Miriam, I was worried stiff!"

In fact, I was literally shaking with fear and it was said more crossly than I'd intended but the unreasonable anxiety was still with me. I looked down at my hands and quickly plunged them into my pockets, to hide the fact that they were trembling. Miriam gently took my face in her cool hands and smiled.

"How could you think I would ever leave you Duncan? I promised you I would always be here waiting for you."

She pulled my face down towards hers and kissed me gently on the lips.

"I love you Duncan."

Her voice faded away and I felt myself being pulled down; everything was black. I was swirling round and round, being pulled further towards something awful as though I was in a whirl pool. And then just as suddenly I was back at Miriam's side and her sweet face, full of concern, was watching me.

"Are you all right Duncan?"

"Yes, yes, of course. Must have had too much sun. I'm fine now, in fact I've never felt better and all because of you. I'm having the most wonderful day Miriam."

Had this girl said she loved me or did I imagine it? It was odd, I felt like telling her that I loved her too but felt it was too ridiculous so I let the moment pass.

In the late afternoon, we passed St. Nicholas Abbey and climbed upwards, through the avenue of mahogany trees, to the top of Cherry Tree Hill where we drank in the view of the east coast. We stood silently, simply enjoying being together; it was silly but I felt so right with this girl, as though we belonged, as though we had known each other forever. I pulled her close, not wanting to lose the feeling and suddenly felt afraid. She fitted snugly under my arm as we watched the orange and reds vie with the blues and purples in the darkening sky. Miriam shivered as though my fear had transmitted to her. I held her closer lifting her chin and then our lips were together in a timeless kiss that seemed to contain the essence of all the embraces I had ever known.

Too soon she broke away, and was running back down the hill before I realised what was happening.

She turned and shouted, "I love you Duncan Stuart, but I have to go home. I'm really late!"
I took off after her but she had disappeared into the trees and the darkness had swallowed her. I searched everywhere, calling her name but it was hopeless; as though the black night had formed a dense protective cloak which had wrapped itself around her and she had simply disappeared. Eventually I was forced to return to the moke and home but I vowed to go back again at first light to find Miriam. The rain fell heavily on the way back and I had to stop to put the hood up on the moke. I had pulled up near Broodhaagen's Bussa, when suddenly there was an almighty clap of thunder. Fork lightning lit up the statue of the slave, arms raised and chains broken. He looked alive.

I hardly slept a wink that night. Miriam had said she loved me and I knew that I loved her too; it was as though I'd spent all my life waiting for this day. I was elated and full of wonder at this instant love. I couldn't wait for dawn when I would find her again.

Early the following day I set out on my quest. When Miriam ran off for home we were at Cherry Tree Hill in the north. She must be known around the area as it was not very populated. I did stop a couple of times as I neared my destination, to ask if anyone knew a girl called Miriam. Stupidly I had not asked for her other name but in any event nobody seemed to know her. I decided to try St. Nicholas Abbey which, as it transpired, was open for tourists. Here I asked the lady guide if she knew a Miriam. She said she didn't but told me if I cared to wait, the owner would be back quite soon and he apparently knew everybody. I decided to join the few American visitors for a tour of the house while I waited.

We roamed the interesting rooms with the guide and spent some

"Bussa"

time inspecting the Wedgewood portrait medallion collection and a lovely old grandfather clock from the year 1800. The house was beautiful and had been kept much as it had been when the plantation was fully operational and slaves worked in the fields. I was fascinated by the relatively new (1936) 'Gentleman's Chair.' The chair had built into it every possible requirement that a reposing gentleman of that era would have needed and I promised myself I would have one made when I reached my old age. In a hallway were valuations of the estate which included lists of slaves, their names, dates of birth and death and how much they had cost. Names like Little Sally and Kitty from 1822 caught my eye, each priced at one hundred and twenty pounds sterling. Not much for a life I thought.

Outside, at the back of the house, I stood under a huge Sandbox tree, where I was offered water in a gourd from a nearby calabash tree. As I sipped my drink, I thought that it was very much as the slaves must have stood, quenching their thirsts, after long hours in the sun cutting cane. I looked over at the old slave quarters and a feeling of such deep melancholy swept through me, as if the pain, heartache and abject misery of all those poor tortured souls was passing through me. The water tasted suddenly bitter and I threw it away. I felt extremely hot, like a furnace was raging through me and catching sight of the Americans disappearing into an old barn, I quickly followed them. Inside a very old film of Bridgetown in the twenties was running. It showed the hustle and bustle of people arriving at the dockside by lighter from ships moored in Carlisle Bay, while fully laden donkey carts trundled by. I watched the scratchy old black and white avidly with its strange jerky movements and then my attention was caught by a girl, sitting at the quayside, dangling her legs. She was wearing a white cotton dress; a small cat sat beside her. I stood up, moving closer to the screen. It was Miriam; there was absolutely no doubt about it. She was sitting exactly where I had found her the previous day with the breeze blowing the same white dress as she looked out to sea. I felt strange, dizzy and peculiar, I stumbled back from the screen and then – nothing.

When I came to, I was sitting in the Gentleman's Chair and the English owner was offering me a cup of sweet tea.

He said, "It's all right old boy, this heat gets to everyone you know. This tea will revive you, believe me."

That much was true. As I drank the sweet tea I immediately felt better. I tentatively asked about the girl in the film. The man replied that she was simply listed on the box as Miriam and asked why the interest.

"It's an incredible tale and quite honestly I'm not sure I understand it myself; I'm very confused, but if you have the time I'll try to explain."

The owner said that with all the tourists gone, he could think of nothing better to do than sit and chat to a fellow Brit.

I told him everything, concluding with my trip to Barbados and what had happened to me since. He listened intently without interrupting once. When the story was finished, the owner took me back to the hall, where the slave names were listed and after searching for a while he discovered what he was looking for. There was Miriam's name. She had died, in the year 1802. She was just sixteen years old. A numbness seemed to be creeping over me as everything felt unreal. I was being spoken to and I was responding but the voices seemed to be coming from inside my head. The Englishman went to an old mahogany bureau where he unlocked and opened the cupboard below. This contained several leather bound volumes and he removed one. Placing it on the desk, he began leafing through the yellowed pages, finally reaching the place he wanted and began to read aloud, stopping occasionally, to make his own personal observations. This was the gist of the story he told:

"In 1802 the plantation was owned by a Scottish family named Stuart who had one son, the apple of their eye. According to these records there had been a terrible scandal that year, when a young slave girl named Miriam became pregnant by the son. Nothing unusual in that old boy, but the son insisted he loved the girl and that he would marry her. This could never be permitted, so after filling their son with some knock out concoction, they shipped him back to Scotland under guard. The rest of the family sold up soon afterwards. Nothing more was ever heard of them.

Miriam, it was written, was beside herself with grief. She took to walking all the way to Bridgetown's dockside and there they would find her looking seaward, expecting her love to return. The new owners brought her back to the plantation several times but then one day shortly before the baby was due, she disappeared altogether. Some say she was last spotted heading for the Animal Flower Cave at North Point. They searched but she was never seen again. Strangely the flowers disappeared from the cave at that time and folklore has it that they will never return until the lovers are re-united. The boy's name was Duncan Stuart."

The Englishman looked up at the stricken face before him.

"What did you say your name was again son?"

EPILOGUE

Duncan Stuart returned to England, sold all his possessions and went back to live in Barbados. He bought the small bar at North Point which brings in enough money for his needs. Duncan spends his time writing and painting but if you really want to meet him, you'll definitely find him in the caves. Amazingly, the flowers have returned again and are a great tourist attraction.

Sarah and Gina have been living happily together in a cottage in the Cotswold village of Burford for the last five years. Sarah has become a very successful artist staging her own exhibitions in London. Gina recently qualified as a paediatrician and works in a small hospital for disabled children, where she can look after her daughter Chantelle, who has greatly improved with the best treatment available in Britain.

IN THE COURT
OF THE CAVE SPIRITS

Here are the caves, quiet and deep.
Here are the spirits fast asleep.
Here lie the souls who wail and weep.
Here lies the girl with a promise to keep.

Who was it dared drive the lovers apart?
Who was it caused her broken heart?
Who was it made life cruel and cold?
Who was it set the death mask mould?

Where is the lover she's destined to meet?
Where is the heart to make her own beat?
Where is the life she took that day?
Where is Destiny? Will she make her pay?

Now he is close and her eyes awake.
Now bring them together for heaven's sake.
Now give her the breath of life she craves.
Now linger as one in the dark of the caves.

Here are the lovers together once more.
Who dares Destiny 'Even the score!'
Where bury the hatred that caused the sin?
Now leave well alone and let love in.

The court is unanimous, the verdict is in.
Who Where Here and Now have absolved the sin.
True love must be innocent the spirits decreed,
Fate has ordained it and Destiny agreed.
Sins of hate, spite and ignorance must always be paid.
But for Duncan and Miriam, all ghosts are well laid.

GLOSSARY OF BARBADIAN SLANG

Bajan	*Person born in Barbados*
Black Rock	*Psychiatric Institution*
Botsie	*Bottom*
Bruggadung	*A crashing fall, loud explosive sound*
Bubbies	*Breasts*
Chupse	*Sound produced by sucking air between the teeth denoting disgust or disapproval*
Deputy	*Other woman; also 'outside woman' or 'squeeze*
Grantley	*Grantley Adams International Airport*
Lady of the night	*Scented night flower. Bot. Brunfelsia Americana*
Limacol	*Cologne or toilet lotion*
Liming	*Relaxing; cooling out*
Mahogany Bird	*Cockroach*
Plantocracy	*Word combining planters and aristocracy*
Stand pon it long	*Ability to maintain an erection for a long time*
Rass'ole	*Arse*
Wicker	*Lesbian*
Wuk-up	*To dance suggestively with hip gyrations*

ABOUT THE AUTHOR

Kay Gillespie is a writer and artist who has travelled extensively and spent ten years living in the Caribbean where she wrote *Tropical Cocktales with a Twist*, and a musical. She has also worked as a photographic model, appeared in commercials and in a hit American TV soap opera.

Kay is now back living in England with her husband and two daughters and has just completed her latest novel, a thriller.

Breinigsville, PA USA
07 November 2010
248818BV00002B/20/A